D1145235

Bad Name Drifter

Sam Galway is settled in Dalton, Kansas, and is now a local dignitary and respected family man. However, Dalton is a town split in two: north of the railroad line life is decent and ordered, but south of the line, cowboys raise hell and the riff-raff of the world frequent the streets.

Into this town comes Sam's younger brother, Wes. Wes has seen action fighting for the Union, and now lives by his wits and his gun. He has also lost the dearest things in life: his wife and son. Wes wants to change his life, but there are complications: there's his nephew who worships him, and his brother who hates him, and he's fallen foul of the town marshal.

A confrontation has to come. Seems like life won't let Wes put down roots, but he won't stop trying.

Bad Name Drifter

Frank Callan

A Black Horse Western

ROBERT HALE

© Frank Callan 2018
First published in Great Britain 2018

ISBN 978-0-7198-2845-4

The Crowood Press
The Stable Block
Crowood Lane
Ramsbury
Marlborough
Wiltshire SN8 2HR

www.bhwesterns.com

Robert Hale is an imprint
of The Crowood Press

Typeset by
Derek Doyle & Associates, Shaw Heath
Printed and bound in Great Britain by
4Bind Ltd, Stevenage, SG1 2XT

1

For eight hours, the land had looked exactly the same. Looking out at the brush and the rocks, and the long vista of a still only half-known territory, his boredom made his eyes search for movement – a cougar, a jackrabbit, a prairie dog – anything to stop him dropping to sleep exhausted. He was ready to talk to himself, and he had gone through all the songs he knew anyway.

He was starting to tire now, with Newton around twenty miles behind him, and he thought he should have stopped there. The Chisholm trail was close, and Ellsworth was not too far, but he had Dalton in his mind and he had been determined to press on. Trouble was, now the dirt was hard in the lines on his face and his belly was rumbling for some food. He could sense that his tough Appaloosa needed some rest, too. He gave in and found a rock to lie against, letting his horse have some time without the saddle.

Would it all work out? He was giving up everything, but the life he had chosen had outlasted its days. Everything moved on, just like folk who moved west and west again. It was the way in this new country that his father had come to, and though he had not moved out of the city, his sons had moved – and moved west. Now here he was, after years of fastening on to every opportunity that was offered, and every chance that was worth a gamble, setting out to change his life.

His reputation was like a paint stain on his coat. It couldn't be moved, erased. He had resolved to be someone else, to do different things, but it wouldn't be easy.

His mind plagued him with thoughts of what kind of reception he would get when he finally reached Dalton. It was ten years since he had seen his brother Sam, and they had never really got along. Big brother was in for a shock. The last he heard, from their old friend Carter the medical man, was that Sam was settled in Dalton, and that was the limit of the knowledge available.

The closer he had come to the town, and thought of Sam, the more his mind went to the faces of his dear wife, Hannah, and their son, Joe, taken from him by the first men whose lives had been taken so he could do what the law refused to do. He had carried that sorrow like a burden that you couldn't unload, and he rarely spoke of it. Yet it was always running through his mind, that ride home, expecting a welcome, his saddle-bags with gifts and his heart full of love. He could be doing things that lifted his mood, and there could be a smile on his face, but inside, the picture of that scene – her lifeless body, with one fatal knife wound, lay as if asleep. He had called her name, shaken her poor body, and then, seeing that death had put his foot on her, he had screamed to heaven in pain. It was all done again when he held what was left of his Joe, too. There was only a limp something, a body with nothing of his beautiful son in it.

He sat there in thought, tormenting himself with what kind of reception he would get from Sam. They had never been close, but then Sam never had any feelings that a person knew about; if he had affections, they were kept locked away in a room only he knew about.

But he was not meant to rest. There was shouting from somewhere close, and he sprang to his feet with his right hand hovering over the Navy Colt. From a point ten feet above, he looked down the other side of the slope and he saw a man sitting on a wagon with hands raised, and two men were pointing guns at him. 'OK, so you're not meant to rest up, Wes Galway. . . .' he spoke to himself, as he did so often. He knew lonesome, like a man could know an ornery sort of pain that hurt every day. He was needed, and he wasted no time, moving silently down the slope, keeping to the cover of some vegetation where he could, eyes fixed on the scene.

7

'So Mister Moran, drop the hands now, and get down here.' This was the taller of the two standing by. The man got down, and immediately was struck so hard across the face that he fell back against the wagon, then was hit again, by the smaller man, and both attackers stood over their prey, laughing.

'Not so sure of yourself now, Moran, hey? Them words of yours is all dried up, mister.' The smaller man, who was dark-skinned as if he had been burned by the plains sun for the last decade, put away his pistol and sat down. The tall man called him Slug and the man replied with, 'What you planning for the paper man, then, Max?'

'That depends on whether he's scheming to be a nuisance to the boss any more or whether he's tired of life.' He chuckled and Slug joined in. Max was spinning his gun around the fingers of his big, solid hand. Everything about him suggested a cowpoke and his accent was Texan.

'I just do my job . . . I relate the news,' their victim said.

'No, you're bending the facts, mister. What you do is throw dirt all over a man's good name,' the man called Slug responded.

It was time for Wes to act, and he stepped out into the light. It was coming to the end of the day, but there was light enough to see the meanness on the faces of the two men who now turned to face him, while their victim lay, barely able to move, in the dust.

'G'day gentlemen. I see you feel very little affection for this poor man?'

'Keep your nose out and move on, feller . . . who the hell are you anyways?' Max spat at the ground, gobbing a mess of chewed tobacco next to his boot. He was tall, all muscle and shine, and full of the wounds of a hard life. His face was perpetually in a frown, and he looked at life as if enemies were around every corner, and some more were in front of him.

Slug laughed again. His partner, Wes saw, only had to pull a face and Slug would copy him.

'I never tell a stranger nothing, mister, particularly strangers like you who are clearly violent types.' Wes enjoyed Max's wry smile. 'See, I never pulled a gun on you . . . I was passing by and I saw that you were treating this gentleman in such a brutal way I had to intervene.'

Now Wes was playing a game. He was teasing them, turning the screw ever so slowly. Confusing the opposition was always a good move. Max asked Slug what to do, and this was a feint. In fact he went for his gun, but Wes's hand was greased lightning and in a split second he ducked to one side as he fired into the tall man's arm. Slug was going to reach for his holster but thought twice about it and froze in fear.

Max was grasping his arm and moaning. Now that Wes could see that the man from the wagon was getting to his feet, it was time to make an exit. He walked to Max and knocked him out cold with a blow to the cheek. Then, as Slug tried to wriggle away, he got the same treatment. The bullet had only chipped at the edge of Max's arm, and it was more burn than wound.

'Ah, peace at last! You are?' Wes held out a hand and the man shook it, smiling. 'Hey mister, I don't know who you are, but I might just owe you my life. I'm Ed Moran by the way . . . of *The Dalton Courier*.' Wes gave a response that showed the man he knew nothing about the paper.

'You not from these parts then, Mr . . .' he asked, still brushing dust off his long black coat. He was every inch the pen-pusher, Wes thought. There was even ink on his cuffs. He was thin, lean and middle height, with cropped fair hair and a very severe, black outfit covering his now stiff limbs.

'No, but I'm on my way to Dalton, so reckon I made a good acquaintance, Mr Moran. Name's not important.'

'I'm Ed . . . call me Ed. I guess the man who saved my life should be on amicable terms, eh?'

'Who are these men? You know them, Ed?'

'Sure I know them. They work for Marshal Argyle.'

'You mean they're lawmen?'

'Since Dalton was swamped by Texans off the Chisholm, and we got the railway, the line between the law and banditry got blurred. It's all down to Argyle . . . and the men in dark suits and darker

10

souls . . . men like Sam Galway!'

A shiver ran through Wes's whole frame. Hearing his brother's name like that sent all kinds of thoughts jabbing at his insides, and his brain worked hard to match his brother with anything criminal. But he held back the questions. It was time to move on to the town. 'Ed, help me get these idiots onto your wagon. We need to fasten 'em up like hogs and take 'em to their marshal.'

Wes brought his Appaloosa around and tied it to the wagon, then sat with Ed Moran to ask some more questions before they reached Dalton. In the back of the wagon, squirming among barrels and packages, were Max and Slug, bound and gagged and burning with hatred for the stranger. Wes had taken their guns and let their horses run off.

'Ed, any man coming to this town needs to know why a marshal's men were attacking a man like you. You a killer on the run?' He smiled.

Ed Moran was weighing up the stranger. Here was a strongly built man, wearing a long coat, pants tucked into high boots, a vest and fancy bandana, with black hair long enough to brush his shoulders, and above all, he was a scarred man. He had maybe grown his moustache and beard to hide some wounds, but he had some on his face – a cheek was pitted and a deep scar could be seen close to his left ear. He wore a Texan hat but he was hard to pin down by his voice.

'No, sir . . . I told you, I run a newspaper.'

11

'Is that a crime?' Wes asked. 'Last I heard it was a good thing. Why were these dogs snappin' at you, Moran?'

'I tend to pull holes in everything Marshal Argyle puts together. Basically, he's supposed to keep the law . . . and by God we need it, with the Texans coming into town at the end of the trail . . . looking for skirts and whiskey. Oh, and a good roughhouse scrap. See, our town is split right down the middle and the railroad track is the border. My job running the *Courier* is to stir things up, to point out where the law lets ordinary citizens down. Well words in print can annoy these scoundrels as much as bullets sometimes. I keep reminding Argyle that he's about as much use as a bow-legged steer . . . Well, mister whoever you are . . . civilization don't end because a coward like Argyle stops trying. His men have been threatening me almost every day for a month. Today I think they would have finished me, if it hadn't been for you . . . That reminds me, what about you? Why can't you name yourself?'

For a few seconds Wes thought about that, and finally, thinking the truth about him would come out anyway when he reached Dalton, he said, 'Wes Galway.'

Moran looked at him afresh, with a different look. A shadow came across his thoughts and he frowned. 'You mean you're. . . .'

'I'm his little brother. Fought for the Union, came out with a few metal souvenirs and holes in my body

12

. . . lived by my gun. Some folk call me . . . The Settler.'

'My God . . .' Ed Moran pulled hard at the reins. The wagon stopped abruptly and the two men in the back had their heads cracked on a wooden crate. 'You're The Settler? Christ . . . I got nothing, mister . . . nothing you want. This is just biscuits and baking stuff . . . and some shirts. Mister, your name is known from the prairies, down the trail to Texas and across to the East. I read about you . . . is it true you turned lawman?'

'I'm trying to start again. Trying not to send any more men to hell. But types like the scum you have here are making my resolve mighty difficult. Drive on, man, I ain't going to slit your throat!'

As they drove on, and came to the outskirts of Dalton, with some strains of a band coming from one of the saloons to their left, and shrieks from men and women letting off steam, Ed Moran's imagination ran riot. He thought of all the pictures he had seen of this man, a supposed gunfighter who had young bucks lining up to take him on. Now here he was about to join his brother, a man with aspirations to run half the world if folks let him.

God help Dalton, he thought to himself, glancing sideways to look at the guns that had taken so many lives, and sure, there were the ice-cold eyes of a killer. The men tied up behind were lucky to be still drawing breath.

They pulled into town and Ed asked, 'Suppose

13

you want to know where your brother lives?'

'No. Hotel tonight . . . I need to clean up, get the stink of the wild off me.'

'Sure . . . well, the Equity is what you want. Tell them Ed Moran sent you.'

'I'll just rid you of your baggage first!' Wes untied Argyle's men and sent them scuttling off to tell their boss about him. There would be trouble that night, for sure. But Wes needed to wash out his innards with some rotgut and wash away half of Kansas from his skin.

Before he reached the hotel, a hundred Dalton folk watched him from their windows and yards. Ed was a news man and he spread the news faster than Wes could walk.

As Wes came near the Equity Hotel he saw the most impressive building in view. It dominated the town like some wooden castle. The whole front extended around a hundred yards, and a stable was included at one side. There in giant letters were the words:

GENERAL UNIVERSAL STORE
SAMUEL GALWAY
You got a need, we got stock and feed

It sure was strange, seeing his name up there, above the street, the name of an important man. The store was massive; big brother had made something of himself, that was certain. What must it feel like, he asked himself, to have your name up there, seen by every passing stranger and every visitor, who would all know that there was a man called Galway here, and he was important. The brother he remembered, though, would have wanted that. He was always wanting attention, always needing to be looked at, admired, told he was worth something. Another kid brother, maybe not so hard-cored as himself, might have resented the elder, and could have let hatred grow inside him, but that was not the way with Wes Galway. No, it would have been a true sign of weakness, and nothing that the world had knocked into him was weak. He had been moulded by the frontier, made strong by the trials of a series of ordeals thrown at him by fate, something more than the weather, and more of a challenge to throw off the trouble fate gave, and move on, determined to succeed.

It was an alienating sensation. Everything he looked at reinforced the sense that he didn't belong. Yet here he was, and this was real. Maybe they would shake hands, have a drink and talk about Ma and Pa. Or maybe Sam would be just as moody and difficult as he was as a child. The mystery and speculation were exciting. He had always been excited by what was new, and now, oddly, here was something old that was now new. It was a brother, and a forgotten one, who was maybe now stranger than a workaday stranger.

Well, Wes thought, *you came a long way from a New*

York back-street, big brother. There was a mix of excitement and apprehension as he thought of the coming day, when he would embrace Sam again, after so long apart.

2

Standing in his bedroom and looking out into the open space of farm land and paddock, Jess Galway was brooding. He had been banished to his room yet again, for answering Pa back in a row over guns. What was wrong with having a pistol? He was fifteen and good as any man. It rankled, that state of still being considered a boy, a child. Why, he had read in the frontier stories about children fighting off the Indian warriors as the savages circled the wagon train. Now here he was, in Kansas, where the fearful Comanches never came, or at least had no reason to come, and he was forbidden the basic arms of a fighting man.

One day he would be out there, in the open prairie, facing a Sioux war-party, or maybe standing in the hot sun, in the dry street of a tough mining town, where men killed each other for silver. Whatever his destiny, it would be with a pistol in one hand and a dagger in the other. But for now, here he was in a room – a room made by a woman, his mother, and not at all the kind of den an outlaw might find himself in. It was a room in a perfectly ordinary home, in a plain Kansas town, where unless you were a few miles further south, the only threat was from the kick of a horse in the stable.

He was in the Galway house, he reflected, and he was meant to grow up and be the next Galway who ran the General Universal Stores, and he would be filling crates with packs of coffee, not cleaning his gun ready for the next shoot-out outside the saloon.

The Galway house was the smartest and fanciest in the town, though it was five miles from the main street. It had a long white wooden porch, with carved arches along between the balustrades, fixed to a red brick core, and three tall chimneys jutted up above the long, round-topped high windows. Galway had created a basement too, mainly for his collection of books and sacred music, and any other old relics he came across, as he saw himself as an antiquary, and was thought to be a scholar by the locals. Sam Galway had built the place to be seen, to be noticed. Riders saw it from a good way off, and they talked about it.

For the son, though, it felt like a jail; yes, it was sturdy and built to last. When Sam Galway first arrived in the area he was planning to move on west, up into Nebraska and maybe Wyoming territory, but he didn't reckon on meeting Lizzie, who never wanted to leave Kansas, and who had been left a great parcel of money enough to last a lifetime.

Jess caught sight of himself in the cracked mirror on his wall. There he could see a man – a slight young man admittedly, in need of some bulk – but a person almost five feet nine, cropped fair hair, a tough face when it had the right expression on it, and bright blue eyes enough to pierce the enemy with an ice-cold stare. But he looked again at his frail build. He looked as though a strong wind would blow him away; he would never be a physically strong man, old Jack Lee had told him, a really strong man has power in his heart. He glanced at the bottom drawer of his desk as he thought about this. In that drawer was his .36 Navy model that Jack had given him. It was twenty years old now, but it was enough if you were in a tight situation. If his pa found it, there would be a leathering.

But for the time being he would have to make do with his periodicals and dime novels, with tales of buffalo hunters, miners and mountain men. They told of a world out west beyond the horizon, well away from the safe streets around him, in north Dalton. He took up his favourite and looked again at the wonderful pictures of the explorers and hunters of days long gone. The pull of wild country was strong in him. Course, he knew that there was always the south town, Loose End the locals called it, where a man could prove himself. One day he would walk in the street down there, two six-guns strapped low on his legs, and chaps over his breeches, shouting out his enemy from the saloon. One day soon. . . .

'Jess . . . time to eat. Come down please, son.' His mother called. He hadn't thought about food at all but now suddenly he felt hungry and his belly felt hollow. He put the stories away and went downstairs.

Lizzie Galway was standing at the table, ladling out soup. 'You've done your penance, sit down, Jess, Your father will join us in a minute. He's writing his speech.'

She was reckoned to be the real belle of the county, but she was only ever seen walking behind Sam, or standing in his shadow. However, she was a striking woman, and her son felt a wonderful maternal power come from her when she was caring for his pa and him. Today the long fair hair, parted down the middle, and combed long, hung over a full house-dress with some folds and frills at the neck. Her body was not adorned except for the bracelet she always wore, one with six diamonds and a silver strap, given to her by Sam on their fifteenth anniversary.

She called for Sam as Jess sat down and kept still, ready for the prayers. He stood up when his father walked in, looking troubled. 'What is it, dear?' Lizzie went to him and put a hand under his chin, then kissed him lightly on the cheek.

'It's this speech. I have to raise the money, Lizzie . . . I have to. Oh, sit down son. I hope you're sorry for that outburst earlier. I don't want to hear from you again about buying you a gun for your birthday.

A man has a weapon, it invites other men with weapons and soon there's anarchy. You need to learn that lesson. I'll buy you a horse, though. Now eat your soup and bread, like a good boy, as soon as we say the usual . . .' They all sat down and Sam spoke the prayer: 'Good Lord we thank you for our daily bread and for all the richness of your earthly dominion, where we have but a short time to stay and praise thee . . . fine, now let's eat!'

Sam was shorter than his brother, but more stocky and heavy; he had the same kind of eyes and hair, similar movements, rapid and nervous when he was in the throes of something important. He had no small talk and found humour a struggle to achieve. Lizzie did her best to keep him sweet and happy. He might preach against violence but, of course, he carried a gun, a pistol strapped high and under his long coat. He had learned that out here you don't look for trouble but if it finds you then you need to reach for the stock of a reliable weapon.

'Sam, if we could help with the speech, we would be happy to. Jess is good with words, my love, as you know.'

Sam brushed across his son's rich, thick hair and managed to seem buoyant, with a comment that Jess had heard a thousand times, 'One day, son, you will be the big man of the GUS empire, and I know you'll be a tough nut to crack, hey?'

'Yes, Father, I will.'

'So no more talk of guns right? You keep to the

book-learning. To be a success in the business world, you need book-learning. Law, history, languages, that kind of thing. Kansas has a way to go before it's in the modern age, but the Galways will help it to get there, right son? Old Jack Lee might have talked up a life of violence to you, but he was way wrong in the head. You see that now, don't you?'

'Sure, Pa.'

The meal was eaten in silence, apart from Lizzie talking about the progress of the quilt she and her friend Elena were making. Her comments brought the dutiful nods from husband and son. But neither of the adults knew how deep was their son's will to escape them.

Wes was checking into the Equity and as he stood at the counter and signed the book, opposite him was the most alluring figure of Emmy Noone, owner of the place. She was an impressive figure, with long curly blonde hair, rich red lips and a shiny necklace around her neck, reaching down to the low-cut neckline of a full-length gown in red and gold, with a neat little artificial rose over her stomach. She asked a lot of questions, but Wes gave nothing away.

'You don't look like a cowboy . . . but you are a Texan, mister . . . oh . . .' She spun the book around and saw the name 'Galway'. She called for someone when she saw the name, and a man came to confer with her. He was much older than her, maybe pushing fifty years, and though he was in a dark suit with a fancy vest, he looked as uneasy in it as a rat in a trap. His hair was slicked back, a rich shiny black, and it was plain that he was part Mexican. He held out his hand in greeting as Emmy said, 'This is Wes Galway. Mr Galway, this is my partner Pete Maleno. He keeps the wolves from the door, and believe me this town is covered in the creatures . . . mostly the human variety.'

'Relative of Sam's I guess?' Maleno asked.

'Brother . . . but he doesn't know I'm here. I been busy in the war and such.'

Ed Moran's information about the stranger had not reached them but it did now, because the newspaperman arrived and told anyone standing near exactly who had arrived. It was too much for Wes, who shunted Moran into a side-room, explaining to Emmy that he would take the key thanks, and he grabbed his roll from the floor, slung it on his back again, and forced Moran to sit down in a quiet corner. They sat down, and before they could talk, Maleno arrived with two whiskies. 'Compliments of the house . . . welcome to Dalton, Mr Galway.'

When they were alone again, Wes gave Moran some words with an angry tone. 'Moran, listen carefully . . . usually I keep my name away from any notice. Do you know how many young bucks come after me, wanting to take me on, walk outside with me, hands over the stocks of our pistols? Too many to count. Now listen, you owe me a favour, so what I want is for you to write about me in your paper, and tell the world of Kansas that I'm done with that other feller in me called The Settler. I'm turning into someone who puts down roots. I'm finished with killing and pain. You see I still got this Navy here, tied still with some cord, but I'm not swaggering around lookin' for a fight. Too many men are lying under the grass because of me. Now please tell them about me ... make me respectable, you see my friend?'

Moran was already reaching for his notebook. 'Fine. So tell me about yourself, Wes.'

They both sipped the whiskey. Wes gathered his thoughts and wiped his mouth. He needed a bath and a wash, and he needed food, but this was more important. 'Moran, fact is, I was brought up back East with my brother Samuel. Real religious we were. I'm Wesley, after the great Christian Englishman. Samuel named after his brother. Well, time passed and the war came along. Off I went, no more than sixteen, and fought against the Confederacy. Got some wounds, cried a lot. Came close to death at Antietam, but then so did thousands more, and thousands more who got took away to the underworld. Then I lived on my wits, veering around the line between the law and sheer hell. It was when I stopped too long in Wichita that I shot dead three men ... men who wanted to kill me and take some dollars I was carrying for a lawyer man. A lot of folk saw me take them on and you know the rest ... when the law let people down, they came to me. One of your newspaper scribblers christened me The Settler. Real humorous eh ... when you think that I never settled any place more than the time it takes to drink a few whiskies and play cards. You want justice when the law ignores you? Ask The Settler. You got a grievance and no lawyer is on your side? Your man been shot down and the law done nothing about it? Talk to The Settler. That was me, my friend.'

Moran was writing in shorthand and keeping up. He was smiling, pleased with such a rich vein of material for his story. 'Now what about your brother Sam? Where does he fit it?'

Wes considered the question. It was maybe wise to say very little. 'Let's just say he missed out on the war and came here, as I now know, to start a good, clean life with an eye to the future of this great state of Kansas. He's got brains. Give him a chance and he'll turn the great Comancheria into civilized life.'

'Well maybe,' broke in Moran, 'but he would need you to face the warriors, eh?' He laughed. Wes thought he had made his brother sound like a coward, when he meant to say he was a man of peace. 'Moran, don't get me wrong ... I'm saying that Sam is a man of principles ... he was always the one with a plan for the future. I guess I drifted.'

'You sure did ... you been the bad name drifter, and that's my piece on you decided ... I'll get busy. Enjoy the Equity, Wes. Emmy has some real juicy women in here!' He went out, eager to have the next

issue of the *Courier* ready for press. It was the best
story for months.

Wes had taken in the feel of the town as he walked
around a little after freshening up. Dusk was close,
but there was enough light to take ten minutes to
cross the rail line and look out over the cattle pens.
There was a stink in the air he knew only too well.
Thanks to papers like Moran's the whole world now
seemed to be informed about the arrival of the rail,
and the following packing of Dalton by the thousands of steers at the end of the Chisholm and ready
to be taken east; it had been a development that hit
Abilene real hard. It was just fifty miles north but no
trail boss was going to worry about the fate of
Abilene. He wanted his stock off his hands and the
dollars in his pocket-book fast as a stuck hog.

Wes stood in the shadow of a barber shop and
looked down the long south street. This was the less
desirable Dalton then; this was the part a visitor
should avoid. There were dance halls and saloons,
and music appeared to be being played some place
every minute. Since he arrived, there had been the
strains of fiddles through the air, and plenty of
yelping and screaming. It was the old story he had
seen so many times. He had been one of the hands,
caked in filth and stink from the long trail over the
wilderness. He had known the thirst that seeped into
a man, that parched heat inside that only one or ten
beers could slake, with something stronger to cut

through the grit in the throat. Now there it was, one of Kansas's Sodoms, living up to its reputation.

He went back to the Equity, feeling good now he was clean and respectable. It was time to ease up and get to know the locals, sound out their feelings about brother Sam before he made his appearance tomorrow. He smiled just thinking about Sam's face when his little kid brother drifted in. But then there was the old wound, of course, and that passed over his thoughts like a dark cloud presaging a storm. That last meeting, as he had ridden off to join the war, had not been a good one. The opposite in fact. It had been his kick back at the hard line Sam had taken since their father had passed away. Wes had been too proud to take any discipline from big brother, a man eight years his senior, with a sense of his own importance broad and heavy enough to sit on life like a buffalo carcass, and just as hard to shift. Well, he thought, Wes Galway was never going to take orders and be goaded to church every Sunday praying to a God who, at Shiloh, was nowhere to be seen and who never lifted the agony of the hundreds of dying men in the fields, taking a slow death for their destiny.

No, Sam could keep his God, and dream all he wanted, but that was his concern and if it made him content with life, then so be it. Wes found a quiet corner and called for a beer. There was a little band playing over the other side, away from the gamblers' niche where three men around a table were

27

growing noisy. The beer came, brought by Emmy, and she gave him a warm smile. 'Man there wants to see you.' She nodded towards the bar, 'The marshal. Don't think he's too happy. Enjoy the beer, Mr Galway.'

'Wes, call me Wes.' She smiled and gave a little curtsey. Then left, with a sway of her body that reminded him what he had not enjoyed for some considerable time. But after his first sip of beer, he was aware of a shadow on the table, and he looked up.

'I'm looking at Wes Galway, I been told? In fact, I'm looking at The Settler. Last I heard about you, seems you were raising hell bounty hunting. I'm Ben Argyle, and I'd like to know why you hog-tied my deputies.' Argyle was squat and broad, with two guns strapped low, and a weather-beaten face. He was every inch the image of a fighter, with face and limbs to prove it. He was around fifty and had an air of boredom about him, as if it was too much effort to lift a drink.

Wes sat forward. He was not happy at hearing those words. 'First, mister, I never was a bounty hunter. Don't believe the rumours that ripple down the trails. Second, I had no idea those men were lawmen. They wore no tin stars. They were beating up a man and appeared to be robbing him . . . or worse.'

'So you were being a good citizen and helping a weak man against the strong. Sure, but I don't like it when my boys get a whippin'. By the way, the man they was questioning was a dangerous radical . . . he's a fraudster and a trouble-maker, so we had a right to treat him rough. Now you hear me. I'm the law here. I don't want no Settler steppin' in to do what the law does. You got that clear?'

'If you're the law, mister, you should be protecting men like Moran. You care for the weak, and you don't leave a space for the evil ones to sneak in.'

'You been a lawman, stranger?'

Already people were wanting to know about him. Keeping private and hidden was going to be impossible. Even this lawman was going to tell everybody that he had a gunman with a criminal reputation in his town. 'I was a sheriff once . . . not for long. Too many men wanted to buy my allegiance.'

Argyle gave a wry smile and stroked his chin, letting Wes know that he was working hard to develop some understanding of a new face around Dalton. 'Well you have been around, and seen some life as well. You in the war?'

'Sure. I've known death and starvation from too close up. Lost my three best partners . . . two on the way to Blackburn's Ford when the war was scarcely started. Somebody looked after me. I expect you were bullying little men and lone men, while I was fighting for a better world . . . for a new nation if truth is told. I seen your kind before, the men who bend the law to suit their greed. My soldiering days taught me more about human nature than a thousand law books. If I had to guess how you got yourself voted into office, mister, I'd say it was with a little fear applied in the right places, am I right? I had friends lookin' out for me in that war, because there was a bond of real friendship, but I bet my last cent that you got no real friends.'

'Well mister soldier boy, they better be lookin' out for you now, because you started on the wrong foot here, makin' an enemy of me. You whipped my boys, and they never leave alone when they been insulted. You understand?'

Wes nodded. Then the man turned and walked out, without another word.

3

It was a fine clear morning when Wes finally reached a spot where he could see his brother's home. There it was, a fine tall place, white, in the heart of a considerable ranch. The white-painted fence stood out, beyond a wide paddock and a few acres that were being tended by a bunch of workers. Around a dozen men were working outside a massive barn, loading materials into a wagon, but none of them stopped to greet him. Wes had to yell out, 'Come to see Sam Galway,' and a big man with broad hands and long hair nodded towards the building. 'In there . . . you here on business?' He put down a box and walked towards Wes.

'No. I'm his brother.'

The man looked, searching Wes's face, before declaring, 'By the saints, I can see him in your face . . . under that hair. I can see it in your eyes, mister.' He screamed something at a boy, who immediately sprinted for the house, shouting out 'Visitor . . . Visitor! Stranger here!'

The big man took Wes's Appaloosa and said he would be fed and looked after. 'Come, I'll walk in with you, mister.'

By the time they reached the fence, Sam, Lizzie and Jess were standing in the porch, moving out into the light. The boy had said that the stranger looked like he'd been in a fight and the family were intrigued.

'This here's your brother, Mister Galway,' the big man shouted, giving Wes a gentle shove in the back and whispering, 'Walk on, friend.' They were soon face to face, and it was an uneasy, difficult moment for them both. For some time, their eyes looked into the other's face, taking in the lines, the marks from life's struggles, the physical evidence of being deep in some kind of fight for life that had taken its toll. But then, after a nervous shaking of hands, Wes seemed to melt into the real warmth that was his real character. 'Brother Samuel . . . I think I need to put an arm around you!' He did so, and Sam slowly loosened from his stiff, formal stance.

'Life has knocked you about, little Wesley,' Sam said, pulling back and looking his brother in the eyes.

'Yeah. Who does it ever leave alone? Though you look mighty well. I see you have a store the size of three normal homes!'

'I do. I built it up with my hands and my brain.

Nobody helped me. I could have used a brother!'

'Sure, and I could have used one seven years back when a bunch of Rebs wanted to make this poor frame leak some blood. But here I am, and I'm paying a social call, like time has never been between us. We're kin and we still have feet on the ground, not under the soil!'

Lizzie and Jess were then introduced, as they stepped forward, and more awkward handshakes followed, after Wes had taken off his hat and given a little bow of the head and said, 'Real good to meet you, ma'am!' Then when it came to Jess, the boy smiled in welcome, thinking how his new uncle was surely an adventurer, a man who had known life way beyond the home that trapped a boy mercilessly. 'Is it true you help the law . . . when it lets folk down, Uncle Wesley?'

'Enough of that, son,' Sam snapped out. But Wes had his answer ready. 'Used to, maybe. Now I'm looking for a different kind of settling! Now I'm just paying a call, ma'am. I don't rightly feel at home in a truly domestic kind o' setting if you follow me? I mean, I'll call again, but I ain't staying and imposing on your hospitality.'

'That's a pity, Wes, as we have three empty rooms here! We don't get much time for social life, and that's a fact. But call in when you like. Jess here needs some new faces, as all he sees is Ma and Pa most days, right Jess?'

'Real good to have an uncle! I been told about

you but . . . well, truth is, I *read* about you. . . .'

'Enough of that son,' Sam cut in. 'We don't want any talk of your frontier adventure tales now.'

Lizzie told everyone to get inside, and there would be coffee and food soon on the table. As for Sam and Wes, they walked, not hand in hand as when they were children, but like two men who have met on a strange track in a foreign land. Sensing the distance, Sam spoke the way he did when there was business to be done. 'Welcome to Gus Haven, brother Wesley.' When they all sat down, and Lizzie had brought the coffees, helped by Jess who took charge of a fine plate of the products of home baking, Wes was quick to speak the compliments. 'Why Lizzie, what a home you have here . . . the smell of cooking, the warmth . . . and your good self, every inch the good wife. Sam, congratulations on what you have done, while I've been rambling and dreamin' . . . that's the plain truth!'

'Uncle Wes,' Jess asked, his mouth half full of cake, 'I read about you in the newspapers . . . you're famous! I got a famous uncle . . . is it all true?'

'Jess, you know how the reporters and the writers, they blow up a story with hot air so much, the truth gets lost somewhere in the mists. Well, my life's been like that. . . .'

'But you . . . you killed men?'

Before Sam could cut in and stop the talk, Wes did it himself. 'Jess, you and me, we'll talk later. Matters such as these, they're not right to speak with women

34

present, especially mothers. We keep these things outside the home, you see?'

Jess saw for sure. He saw the Colt under Wes' long coat, and he saw the high boots and the vest, and the little bow tie at his uncle's neck. Most of all he saw the scars. Suddenly on another dull day, a man from the myths and legends of some distant world had walked into his own little home.

Sam was curious to know about that lost period, the years apart. He pushed for more information. 'Brother, yes, course I lived by the gun, but you see I had what you've got, and it was taken away.'

'Land?'

'No, nothing so trivial. I don't speak about this, Sam. It was a while back . . . I was down in the Pecos and I had me a wife, Hannah. She had been an orphan. We were both movin' around with nothin' much in the way of a plan. But we built somethin' no more than a shack, part sod-house really. Then we had a son, Joe. He was a beautiful boy, Sam. I wish I could have brought him here with me today, to meet his fine cousin. Well, one day I left them at home to find more work. I was away half the day . . .' He was finding it hard to talk, but carried on, with the emotion welling up in him. 'When I came home, Hannah was lying on the floor of the lean-to. A knife was in her chest. Then inside, my boy was on his back, shot through the chest. Blood had turned his little shirt a dead brown. Could have been asleep . . . Wasn't Comanches. They would have taken my boy.'

'Then who was it, Wesley?' Sam asked, while Lizzie reached an arm across to her new-found brother-in-law and squeezed his hand.

'Sam, down in that border country, there is evil comin' at you like a bad wind. The legions of bad men, ruthless outlaws, plunder the place, and it's real huge ... too long and endless ... the mind can't take it in. Well one of these bad winds scorched through my loved ones that day. Could have been most likely the Comancheros, the scum of the worst level of humanity you can imagine. So you see, I had plenty of reason to be mad at the world. But Sam, let's turn to you, big brother, what do you do to turn a dollar?'

It didn't take long for Sam to move into a lecture in answer to his brother's questions about the GUS store and the ranch. 'Good of you to call it a ranch, Wesley. Fact is, I sell things, anything folk want. When you ran off to war, I came west. Meant to head over to Nebraska, try mining. I read about the silver there. Well, this beautiful woman was in the way, and I'm sure glad she was.' He reached across and squeezed her arm, then went on, 'So I had to make a living, and you know that Pa back in New York started with selling from a barrow ... well, I bought what I could and I sold what I could ... the result, after some years mind, was my store, and my place here in Dalton. Kansas is a real fine place to be, brother. I got twenty acres of it, and I sold some. The Homestead Act set me off good. Now I'm pushing for big change. I want this town to be more than a few square miles of cattle stink and drunken Texans. Politics, Wesley, politics is my future. I'm thinking grand scale, you follow?'

Wes did a lot of nodding, and he kept his thoughts to himself. The brother he had known so long ago was not visible across that table. He had gone deep into the man opposite, lost somehow. When Lizzie and Jess left them to talk more freely, Sam brought matters around to the difficult subject of his brother's 'lost life', as he called it. 'Wesley, I need to know. Is it true, about the killings and the Settler business?'

'Stretched, like hearsay always stretches things, Sam. Sure, I helped people when they was kicked down, when they was ignored. You see, when I look back at my life, after the war mainly, I see injustice. Little men pressed down, shouldered out, ignored by the law . . . most places don't have no law, and by the way, you need to get rid of that excuse for a marshal you got here.'

Sam was skilled at keeping his genuine thoughts well out of hearing. All he could say was, 'Maybe you misjudged the man on small acquaintance, brother?' There was no answer.

'Well, Wesley, stay as long as you like. You have plans?'

'One. Just one. I plan to find something respectable – a life where everyone has forgotten that reputation. Your press man will help me, I think.

He's printing something to help me be more understood and less despised.'

When he heard those words, Sam was visibly holding back a rage inside. His face flushed red, and his fist clenched as he struck the table. 'Press man? You refer to the dealer in lies and insults, Edward Moran? Well he's destined to leave this town, and I'm going to have him ridden out. If he refuses, he might find that he's behind bars, Wesley. Have nothing to do with that viper, you hear?'

'He's a good man. I met him.'

'He's the spawn of Satan, Wesley. I forbid you to have anything to do with that man!

'You *forbid* me! Well here's that big brother back again, the one I used to know, who bullied me and everyone else he could! I thought I'd found a different man but you're just the same pig-headed idiot that tried to push me around. Here you are, full of hatred, as usual.'

Lizzie rushed into the room, calling out, asking what was wrong. Her husband was fighting back the urge to take a stick to his brother and beat him black and blue, as he had done on more than one occasion back home. He had just stood up and raised an arm when she came in and stared at him. 'This brother of mine would have the Texan scum take over the town. Yes, he would have the radicals on the hustings, preaching anarchy! Why did you come here, Wesley, why?'

Wes got to his feet and spoke calmly, 'I'm so sorry

ma'am, as you have been so hospitable, but I feel that I can't stay here with the prig and bully I knew back home. You'll find me at the Equity of you want to speak to me.' He went to grab his coat and hat, and walked out of the house, apologizing again.

At the porch, as Wes walked towards the stable, Sam shouted out, 'You're a drifter, brother Wesley, a no-good drifter, and with a bad name that sticks to you like sweat to a whore! You hear me . . . you're in The Lord's back yard . . . He's lost you!'

Wes never even reached Dalton. He pitched down somewhere in the open, lit a fire and then slept under the moon, bitterness eating at his soul like some ravenous vermin. Maybe being a free roving sort was better after all, if that's what being civilized made you. Out here, he had the moon, the freshening wind, and the call of the coyotes and wolves. There was no contamination by humankind out here, and he sensed, not too far away, the men of the tribes, the kings of the Comancheria and the northern plains, holding their own, while the great new metal horror of the railroad was heading relentlessly out to their fenceless homes. It would be bringing folk like his hard-hearted brother, men fixed only on profits and revenues, at the expense of the heart.

Back in Dalton, after a cold dawn and some hours of eating and knocking out the effects of the night's whiskey, Ben Argyle, Max and Slug managed to get together and deal with the salt in their wounds named The Settler. They sat in the jail office, sipping strong coffee and ignoring the drunk in the nearest cell who was demanding food. Ben Argyle was so sore at the attack on his boys that he launched into a monologue and the deputies could hardly say a word. 'He comes here, into my patch of Kansas, and he wounds my first man, and then he sits in the damned hotel and looks at me bold as a rat gnawin' on a dead hoss and he makes eyes at Emmy . . . well that's enough to get him a life sentence or a one-way ride to hell. . . .'

He was a man carrying plenty of excess weight. When folk reached for a way to describe him to visitors, they compared him to a bull; he was never known to smile, and he was generally distinguished by a slight limp, the result of an accident back in his youth when he had been one of the Texans on the trail from the distant South. He had learned his fighting skills working with the raiding parties from the Red River, out for Indian scalps, thirty years back from his new life with his high status and his wish to forget what he once was.

Argyle was sore at the world. He had moods like that, more and more often these days. Something rubbed him up the wrong way, well he would go and look for a way to cause pain somewhere. Now he was out to shake up the whole town and make it pay for the fact that a stranger had blocked the attack on Moran. *I'm aimin' to shake 'em all at the throat*, he said to himself. He wanted the whole place in his grasp.

He wanted to be the one with the grip on the wind-pipe. Somebody want to breathe? Well ask Marshal Argyle nicely now. All the little nasty ways of squeezing these tediously decent townsfolk were about to be applied. He would have their cash; he would have their nodding heads and no arguments, and most of all he would have their cash and their land.

The drunk screamed out for food. He was ignored. Then Max managed to say, 'By the way, my arm hurts . . . skin wound maybe but boss, it sure stings and burns like I never knew . . . you gotta fix this man.'

The drunk called out again. This time, Ben walked across, picking up a rifle on the way, and then rammed the stock through the bars and into the drunk's jaw. He yelped and fell back. 'Go give him some sleep, Slug,' he commanded, and Slug went in to knock the man into unconsciousness.

'Now, question is, how? How we aim to settle the Settler boss?' Max asked.

The marshal put his feet on the table and then shoved some baccy into his mouth. He gave himself a while to chew it and show his pleasure, before he announced, 'There's a few thousand head of steers due in any time now, and we've got some special police recruited, boys, as always. Well who's the meanest beast with a six-gun, Max? You know, the chief lawman in that crowd?'

Max smiled so that his yellow teeth stood out from his dirt-ingrained face, and he said, 'Bill Brady!'

'Yep, Mr William F. Brady. You know what Max, I

can see into the future. I got a very special talent. I can see that Wes Galway is fated to make an enemy of Bill Brady. Yes sir, and someone might get hurt!'

Bill Brady was a name that had spread a degree of fear from Atchison to the Colorado border. Some said he was a bounty hunter; others insisted that he was rich from hunting buffalo and was close friends with the Nez Perce. He had traded with the Sioux, they said, and survived the war, where even the hell that was Gettysburg was an ordeal he survived. He worked alone, but was hired to lead the Specials when there was a threat of disorder. He was just the man the suits and bow ties of Dalton needed now that Jim Cash's steers were on their way, goaded and bullied by scores of wild Texans ready for trouble.

The lawmen laughed, relishing the thought. Brady had reputedly killed fourteen men in gunfights. That was why he was the perfect man to lead the special policemen when the cowhands came to town, ready for mayhem and plunder. 'This is gonna be some spectacle, boys. Sit back and watch!'

4

In the Harmony Hall, in the cleanest, smartest end of Dalton, the audience were packed in, every seat full, and the important guests seated at the front, served with drinks and fussed over like prize stallions, as most of the decent folk of the town waited for Sam Galway's speech on the proposed line to Wichita. Wes arrived late, after booking in again at the Equity and cleaning himself up. A solid breakfast had been eaten and he was feeling good, but ready to see his brother at his most strange and distant – the public speaker. Yes, he was not disappointed. Sam walked on, following an older man, who pointed to a seat where Sam sat down. Then the older man walked forward and spoke.

Wes sensed someone coming to sit by him, and there was Jess, dressed so smart he could have been a lawyer, looking up at him and beaming with pleasure. 'G'day Uncle Wes. Shame about you and Pa having words.'

'We always did, son. Our words were always like the North and the South . . . close up but never like to get on.'

After the old man introduced him, Sam stood up and flapped his hands to subdue the applause. 'Thanks ladies and gentlemen. I appreciate your warm welcome. You may recall that I spoke here in the Harmony about six months back, after the Council were to meet with the railroad managers. Well, everyone there liked the notion of a line to Wichita. Now, a little further down the road to progress, it will happen – if we can raise dollars through bonds.' He paused a while and there were a few shouts of disagreement, mainly by folks who hated parting with their money. But he spoke again. 'Good people of Dalton, I have to speak directly to you now, if you will allow it . . . you see, I came here meaning to move on west, but truth is, I came to love this county. Yes, it became a forward-looking place, with dreams and aspirations, and I like that . . . I want to be a part of the dreams you good people cherish. Will you allow me to do that?'

There were loud cheers and screams, and his name was yelled out. Someone said, 'Sam Galway for President' and there was general laughter. Then he waved a hand and they listened afresh. 'Good people of Dalton, we have made all the right things here for a good, decent family life. We made schools, we made a church, we made decent hotels and liveries . . . we have the mail, arriving safe most times. The war that almost sent its poison through the entire land is now far behind us, and the next step is to open up this vast new country . . . with the iron rail! Fact is, we need everyone here to buy bonds . . . and you can put your dollars down today at the table near the door as you leave, and walk away with certificates, proving that you have invested in that dream I spoke of. . . .'

There were more shouts, but when the row faded, a threatening voice was heard. 'You spoke about the war, Galway, but you never picked up a gun, right? What fightin' have you done for this golden future of ours?' A few more voices of dissent cut the air.

Sam was calm. He waited for quiet and gave a measured reply. 'Sir, you can speak your mind. That's only fair. But see, I fought here at home. Not every war means bullets and bayonets . . . no, it can want strong arms and determination to build peace and . . . make a life for women and children . . . like my son for instance . . . where are you . . . stand up, Jess my boy!'

Jess got to his feet but could not really be seen. Wes held him firmly at the waist and lifted him up into general view. There were more shouts and whistles, all approving of the family man who seemed to represent the best of their world.

The officials were placed at the door and, sitting at a long table, took the money and wrote down names. Sam stood at the end, by the door like a preacher on Sunday after the sermon, where he smiled and shook hands. After some time, filled with gushing words and hearty congratulations, there was no one left in the room except Jess and Wes. The officials thanked Sam, and took the money away to a secure safe in the town bank.

'Wesley, I have to thank you for that. It was such a shame we didn't see eye to eye about the newspaper man. You'll see him for what he is in the broad daylight of common sense.'

'No, I sure will not. See you later, Sam. I'll call again soon.' He walked off, in need of a conversation with the newspaperman in question.

It was a hot, dry day in early summer, and the town was peaceful, even sleepy. But in the offices of *The Courier* there was a feeling of desperation and frenzy. Ed had spoken to a rider who had come into town and been told that the drive was only a day away. The southern boys would soon be letting go and shooting at shadows in Loose End. It was always a good story, and needed preparation. But there was something else going on when Wes reached the office door and paused to listen before knocking. Emmy Noone was not happy, and she stood at one side of the office while Ed Moran sat at his massive desk, listening to her, trying to stay calm.

'Ed, I've known you a long time . . . this piece on The Settler . . . it's going to bring every spotty youngster between Topeka and Wichita to the place, looking to prove themselves . . . looking to put some

46

lead in Wes Galway. Can you imagine the hotheads and bandits reading this? Where will they gather? Why, at my hotel!'

'Well it's in print now. I can't go back. You got the first copies. Nobody's seen it yet apart from you and the marshal maybe.'

Wes knocked at the door and stepped in. Emmy Noone looked slightly embarrassed. She knew he had heard her words. But Ed Moran was not at all troubled. He stood up and went to shake Wes's hand. 'We were just talking about you . . . here, the *Courier* has just come off the press. I've done the piece about you . . . you know Miss Noone I think?' Wes nodded and took off his hat.

'I heard you. I can see that you think I'm going to spread dirt on your clean town, Miss Noone, but believe me, I'm not the man I was. Ed here is going to help me change into more of a steady and easy kind of man . . . if I can do it. I gave him my story because maybe folk will help me, give me a chance.'

'My Pete says you can't, I'm afraid to say,' Emmy said, lowering her voice now. 'Sorry to dash your hopes, but everybody in this town has seen the pictures of you and to them you're a desperado. You're a killer. But you're welcome at the Equity as long as you keep out of trouble. I believe that a man should have a chance to reform and maybe even change. You know why, Galway? Because I'm in the same frame of mind, to be frank. You see, this town could be the model of a new kind of community, given a

47

chance. I've been down there, with the servants, the bartenders, the fieldworkers . . . oh yes, I've worked hard for all I've got. Me and Pete, we joined up and used the savings we had to buy the Equity. Now it's not the classiest place to lay your head or sit and have a drink, but it's not a spit and swear saloon bar. Sorry to say that your presence might bring things down to the dirt again. But I'm willing to give you a chance . . . when I came in here I was mad as hell, but now I'm thinking you're worth a bet. I hope you prove me right, Galway.'

'A fine speech, Emmy. You should write for my paper,' Moran said, offering them both a drink. But Emmy turned it down and left, with some last words. 'Just keep your head down, Galway.'

'Wes. You can call me Wes.' He tried a smile but met with no response. She went out, leaving him with no notion of how she felt about that, and her parting shot was, 'Never known such a naive man . . . nobody here's givin' you a chance!'

Ed Moran and Wes had that drink, and Wes read the piece on him, sitting quietly while Ed threw out commands to the workers in the next room. When he came back in, Wes said, 'Thanks Ed. That should help. You say here "Wes Galway wants to succeed like his respected brother Sam, as a valuable member of this community. The editor begs you to give him a chance." I like that. It might just make an impression.'

Wes left Ed to his work and decided to test the

ground. What better way to do that than to walk into the GUS store and let folk see him doing something plain ordinary? He walked in, flapping his long coat over his belt and gun as usual, and started looking at the line of glass display cabinets down one side. Some local people were at the counter, and their heads turned. They whispered something and he heard 'The Settler' spoken very quietly. He turned to inspect the cabinet and there were boots, bottles, jars and even some periodicals on the top shelf, all under glass. Then he saw another cabinet, packed with women's items, and his gaze fastened on a cameo brooch on top of a neat little box. He turned to look at a man who sat by the doorway, watching everything that moved. In seconds, the man was across to Wes, ready to help. He was around fifty, carrying too much weight, and squeezed into a dark suit.

'This brooch . . . I'll take it.'

'Fine . . . very nice thing, for your lady I suppose?'

'He ain't got no lady . . . he's the drifter in the paper, Henry.' A woman's voice called out from the far end. 'But he's Galway's little brother!' There was more whispered talk.

'Well, Mr Galway, you have excellent taste. This is the goddess Diana . . . with a spray of flowers and a white dove . . . very tasteful, Sir. I'll box it up for you. Is it a gift?'

It was. It was for Lizzie. No sooner had the man wrapped the cameo and handed it to Wes, who gave him the twenty dollars, than the whole crowd of shoppers lost their interest in Wes and ran to the door, shouting for Henry to look who was in the street.

Wes joined them. It was as if a detachment of the army had arrived. Ten men on horses, trotted up the main street. The first thing a person noticed was their armaments: all had rifles and more than one six-shooter. They were dressed in black jackets and brown breeches, all well armed and mostly whiskered and thick-set as if wrestling was their game. Leading them, riding a grand strong chestnut Morgan was a broad-set man with long black hair with a long and shaggy coat on him. He raised an arm and they all dismounted.

Standing behind the crowd by the door, Wes heard, 'The police . . . looks like we got the wild boys on the way,' and 'That's Bill Brady . . . he'll stand no nonsense from them cowboys!' Then the excitement died down as the police went into a building over the street, leaving the mounts with some hostlers who had come out to help. As the shoppers went back to their counter and had goods wrapped, Henry explained the situation as Wes made ready to go. 'You see, Mr Galway, that there man at the front, he was William Brady. You heard of him? No? Well he's been here before. Comes to round up the drunks and the fighters when they get out of control. Reckon they bounce off him in a set-to. He's thicker than a dry hay-bale and it would take a storm at sea to blow him off a straight line. More than useful with a gun o' course. Anyways, enjoy the cameo, Sir.'

It was turning out to be an eventful day. But now, with the small army of lawmen filling the town, and the talk of the cow punchers coming in to let off steam, there was a distinct air of unease about the place and he could sense it as he made his way back to the hotel. Heads turned as he walked. Some people held their copies of *The Courier* as they stared. Never before, in all his travels, had he felt so much like a curiosity on show at a fair. Never before had he been so exposed to public discussion and interest. His instinct was to find a hole and hide. But he had forgotten one thing in allowing the paper to publish this account of him. Some folk in Dalton wanted him to stay as The Settler, and one of these was waiting for him at the Equity.

Wes walked straight to Pete and Emmy, who were watching their domain from the welcome desk, and this time Emmy had a smile for him. Wes managed a joke, 'Now Miss Noone, I'm just here for a game of poker and some friendly chatter.'

She winked at the waiter and said, 'A beer will be brought to you, Sir! Over there, because the lady wants to speak to you. She owns around a third of the whole county. I heard she needs a manager for her working horses if that's your skill, now you're on the right side of the law, Wes.'

'Or maybe she needs something more ... intimate, I think. She's very lonely, they say,' Pete added, with a wry smile.

Wes glanced across and saw a youngish woman, dressed as if she had wealth and status, sitting in an armchair by a low table. He went to her and she held out an arm. For a minute he felt he ought to kiss it and bow. There was something regal about her. She was maybe only around thirty, with auburn hair in curls, reaching down to her slender shoulders. There was a slight hint of amusement from a crease at the corner of her mouth, and her white gloves were on the table, leaving her bare hands to show their delicacy as she folded them on her knees and sat very still, watching him intently.

'I am Lydia Steiner. You are the man I need to speak to ... on business. Emmy tells me that you are a man of business and that you're looking for something to keep you busy.'

'I could be. If it's the right kind.'

'Do sit down.' She gestured towards the armchair opposite. Her movements were graceful, mannered. Everything she did stood out, and she was wearing so many clothes, mostly laced and delicate, with a high collar on the chemise, that her real beauty under all the materials was not easily seen. But Wes could tell, by instinct, that she was a special breed of woman; he had met them before, and had always tipped his hat to them and made way as they walked by him. The smile of welcome never left her face as he stood there, in thrall to her. He had a feeling that something in her made men do what she wanted. For now, he was happy to do the same.

She waved an arm, beckoning him closer. 'Sit . . . you make me nervous.'

His beer arrived and finally he relaxed a little.

'Excuse me for saying this, ma'am, but you act like there should be a servant standing behind you. You a European lady, with a Lord somebody in tow?'

'No, I'm merely a woman who enjoys a degree of style, even in this God-forsaken backwater. But sit down, I have work for you if you want it.'

He sat and moved an arm to take a pull of the beer. Before he could even take a sip, she said, 'I want you to kill the man who made me a widow.'

5

It was late, and the town should have been quiet. At the Equity Pete Maleno was cleaning tables and Emmy had gone to catch up on some chores, and the bar was left for the staff to tend to. There were only a few men playing cards in a corner, and some drunks at the bar who had been asked to drink up. Pete was looking forward to a quiet game of cards and for some time to think over the proposition from the European lady, as it had been a long day, and his energy had been used up, checking the strangers who turned up, from the trail, keeping out any rowdies and letting in the loners and more manageable men.

Then in came Max and Slug, with two other men behind. They called out his name and then, as he came over to them, Max kicked a table over and the men behind started smashing a mirror and throwing bottles onto the floor. Pete was reaching for his rifle behind the counter, when Max cracked his fist on

Pete's face and he toppled back, sprawling helplessly against a line of chairs.

'Oh hell, Slug, see what can happen when a bunch of wild roisters start kicking up the dust? A real nice establishment can git broke. Shame. . . .'

Pete was on his feet now, standing in front of Max. 'What do you want, Max? Get to the point.'

'What do I want? Well now, I'm here to help, and all you can do is turn nasty on me. That's not a friendly tone to take, you little scum Mex. Point is, I'm here on business. You have to consider what might happen to this very smart place if say a bunch of cowpokes came in raising the Devil from his slumber? How could you stop them burning the place down, Pete? I mean one little greasy Mex against a dozen tough characters with guns and bad moods? It surely would be worth your while taking out insurance.'

'Get out of my hotel, Max. Get out!' Pete snapped, facing up to him. But a fist slammed into the side of his face and when he hit the floor, a boot pressed on his face. Then two men dragged him up and held him as Max jutted his face up close to Pete's and said, 'Listen, a hundred dollars a month. That's the insurance cost, payable to the marshal. I'll collect it every last Friday. You got that? Otherwise, well, this place could catch fire or it could blow up. These are dangerous times.

'Leave the man alone.' A voice came from the card players in the corner. Max's response was to draw his pistol and fire a shot at the man who had stood up offering help. The bullet hit his arm and he fell back with a cry of pain.

'First collection next Friday then, or who knows what could happen.'

They walked out, leaving Pete bruised and sore. As he sat back to find some support, Emmy appeared at the head of the stairs and called out, asking what was the noise? He explained that he had thrown out some drunks.

'You've read about me them ma'am? I think you didn't read with the right degree of attention.' Wes didn't like the fact that this clearly very wealthy woman thought he was something to purchase, to own. 'I guess you think you're able to corrupt a saint, Mrs Steiner?'

She allowed her expression to soften and leaned forward. 'Wes Galway, I did read the piece about you, and I did pay attention. I know you're looking to find a new life, and that's my offer. Maybe I was a little too bold and raw in asking you to kill somebody. The truth is, I need a man about the place to run everything.'

'So murder would be part of the job I reckon? That your drift?'

'Let me be frank, Wes, if I may call you that . . .' He nodded. 'There's a man in this town who had my brother beaten almost to death, and it was the same sick soul who drove my husband to despair . . . Wes, the truth is, my man took his own life, bullied and pressured to it by this ruthless son of the Devil . . . and now my brother, he lies down most of the day and when he can manage it, he hops around on crutches, all because of this man. You know who the culprit is?'

'How could I?'

'Marshal Ben Argyle.' She paused to watch Wes's reaction, then carried on. 'He wants my land. Simple as that. You heard about the railroad to Wichita? Well my land is not directly any kind of obstacle, but it's close, and Argyle wants it as it's the best land around for building all the modern horrors that come with the rail. Oh yes, basically, he wants another town there. It's just ten miles north. You do believe me don't you?'

'I'm trying to take all this in, ma'am. You're saying that the law is corrupt, that the man who should be on your side is your deadliest enemy?'

'That about says it all.'

'You read that I was The Settler, and that I put right what the law wouldn't help with. I see. Now, here I am trying to be a decent person, not living by gun and fists, and you want me to. . . .'

'I want a man around . . . a strong man, one who can use those fists and that gun, and it strikes me that you're one of the very best! Please say yes, Wes Galway.'

'Well I sure ain't aimin' to kill a man like some bounty hunter. Anyway, I won that reputation by

trying to put things right for people . . . for victims
. . . when the law let them down. That's not the same
thing as takin' a life for vengeance.'

'Fine Mr Galway, let's just say I need a man with
some presence, someone who gets things done.'

He thought for a moment. His resolve to rub out
his past life was not doing so well. But this could be
a decent way to move on, at least till he had time to
think things through. It was an offer of a job, and he
needed one. It would give him a home, near to Sam,
and offer a chance to be a part of the Dalton community. He had seen Max and Slug try to do their
dark business on Ed Moran, so what she said could
be true. His hand tapped on his gun, with a slight
indication of guilt that he was stepping backwards,
but he said yes. Lydia embraced him and called out
to Emmy, now standing at the bar after the trouble,
who was her oldest friend in town, to bring her best
bottle of brandy across.

Ed Moran was a long way into the southern part of
town, deep into the chaos and disorder of Loose
End. He was there to write the feature he had done
so many times – the arrival of the Texans and the
cattle whose noise and protests filled the air denser
than a rain storm. He sat on the porch of the Wild
Comanche saloon and scribbled his notes, as Bill
Brady stood behind, watching his men line up along
one side of the street, where they stared threaten-
ingly at the massive scene of frenzied business before

them, where cowboys busied themselves guiding the cattle into the vast pens, and the bosses shouted at them. Behind all this there was the railhead and all its supporting buildings, and then there were the saddlers, the smiths and the provision merchant. Already the medical men were trotting their buck-boards into view to his left. The worst effects of the long trail from way down south at Donna or San Antonio meant that the men would arrive with any number of complaints and ailments, and they were in need of any kind of help, from dentists to eye-doctors, and of every kind of treatment from being de-loused to having boils lanced. When this was all sorted, they would hit the saloons with their partners who, clear of problems, had been first to the whiskey.

All this, everything he saw and heard, was copy for his newspaper feature. The good people north of the line might fear and despise the Texans but they loved to read about them. It was the same reason why the gentleman in the suit and tie needed to read about the mountain men in his Sunday periodical.

But Ed did not have his time to concentrate on this for too long. Bill Brady, behind him, sipping a beer and irritating the newspaperman like a fly on a horse's eyeball, was wanting to be the hero. 'Just say that Commander William Brady brought in his noble band of fighters to ensure that peace was pre-served. You got that, pen-pusher?'

Ed had to put on a front, pretending that Brady

was taking the headline. He nodded and smiled every time Brady said anything. Then the big lawman lit a cigar and waved it close to Ed's ear as he sat there, writing, and it was all becoming too uncomfortable when two cowboys saw him and ran across. They didn't like what he was doing and one swung a fist at him, knocking him back off the chair. It was the excuse Brady needed to let loose his bad temper. Some demon in him always wanted to be causing pain, and before Ed could get to his feet, Brady had the two cowboys on the floor. He knocked one clean out cold with a blow to the temple, and then he shoved the other to the dirt and put his huge foot on the man's chest. 'You annoying my friend Mr Moran? Yes you are, you scum. Now have a face-full of this.' He lifted his foot and kicked the man straight in the face, and then hit him again with his rifle stock. Both cowboys lay still as corpses. They might have been corpses, for all Ed knew. He had had enough, and he scrambled to his feet and ran back home quicker than a jackrabbit dodging bullets.

Sam Galway had taken to his sick bed. More often than he liked, an old illness came back to trouble him these days. It was always the same kind of fever, with sweats and dizziness, and all he could do was to take to his bed. Lizzie became his nurse and she was very good at it. As she leaned over to wipe his forehead with a warm cloth and soothe him, Sam told her again how much he needed her and how she was the best wife a man could want. 'Lizzie ... what would I do without you? You're the strong one in this house. The world out there don't know it, but you keep everything together, lady!'

She was telling him to sleep and stop trying to talk, but he was worrying. There were meetings with the bank, and there was new stock to catalogue. But she made him sip hot coffee and spoke of all the things he liked, all the good things to get better for. But what Sam didn't know was that Jess was taking advantage of the situation.

If ever there was a relaxation of his father's regime, Jess would make a bolt for freedom, or engage in activities that were forbidden. When Sam was away from home, Jess would creep into the study, as he knew where the door-key was stowed, and take the Starr Arms revolver from the cabinet drawer where his father kept it; he loved its feel and weight, and he would steal out and go to the limits of the GUS ranch, where he practised his shooting. The workers knew what he was up to but he bribed them to keep their mouths shut. Talk around the place was that Master Jess would step into trouble one day, or, '*Master Jess is one hell of a shot with that thing.*'

Sam Galway finally slept, early in the afternoon, and Lizzie went back to her cooking. As soon as Sam was well enough, she was planning on meeting her friends down in Dalton, where she had a cultural circle, mixing with the finest ladies of the county;

they would discuss the latest news and fashions, sometimes engage speakers and generally enjoy time away from their men and their chores. She was thinking about all this when she heard one of the hands shout from the gate 'Brother's here again!' She went straight to the door, walked out and gave Wes a smile as he left his horse with a hostler and came to say howdy.

Inside the house, Lizzie explained about Sam's illness and brought coffee as the two of them sat down and Wes knocked the dust off his breeches, and then apologized. 'Hell, I didn't think . . . I am sorry Lizzie. I'm not accustomed to being in an actual *home* you see!'

'I can see that, Wes. But don't worry. I have a brush.'

'Lizzie, I brought a little somethin' for you. I been told that womenfolk like pretty things, right?' She agreed, and the package was handed to her. Lizzie took a penknife and cut open the package. When she held the cameo in her hand, a warm, delighted smile of pleasure spread across her face and Wes blushed slightly as she thanked him and pecked him on the cheek. 'You're the kind of brother every man should have!'

'Well now, I lost my woman . . . so I reckon I need to take care of my brother's good wife, keep her safe. I was made to protect, though I failed in that regard with my own dearest.'

'It was not your fault, Wes. You said it yourself. It

was a bite from a monster stretching over that land. There was nothing you could have done . . . you were finding work to feed those loved ones!'

Lizzie hugged him close. 'Wes, think of yourself as my brother. I always wanted one. Now, what are you doing with your time? I hope you're looking forward, not back.'

He explained about his new post with Lydia Steiner, and he soon saw that Lydia and Lizzie were friends. They usually met at the discussion afternoons, but there had been a problem. 'That's good news, Wes,' she said. 'Lydia hasn't been to our cultural talks for a while . . . we all heard about the difficulties with her poor brother. Such a shame about her husband. He took ill a while ago. It was a very sad decline, Wes. Poor man took his own life while in drink. They say it was the pressure of running the whole of the ranch and business.'

She appeared to be unaware of Lydia's accusation of Marshal Argyle. He could see that something was bothering her, and he guessed it might be Jess. When he asked where the boy was, she said, 'Out there some place.' Wes offered to go and find him.

The workers outside knew exactly where young Jess was, and their nods indicated the place where the shots were coming from. When Wes turned a few corners, past stables and barns, and there was Jess, standing in the gunman pose, right hand steady over the holster strapped to the leg, and then he moved and in a blink, three bottles ranged along a fence

63

were hit and shattered. Wes clapped and Jess turned, a look of fear on his face.

'Uncle Wes! You came!'

'Sure. Shake hands, mister. Good shootin' – what you got there?'

Jess held out the gun. 'Starr Arms . . . Army . . . I used to have one, Jess. It's a fine weapon. Your father approve?'

Jess flushed with a communication of considerable guilt.

'I won't say nothin', little nephew. Just keep the bullets to bottles hey, not at people!'

Jess filled the chambers again and handed it to Wes. 'You do it, Uncle Wes. . . .' He ran to line up six bottles and then ran back. Wes took out his own gun and lay it in the dust, then slipped the Starr Arms in place. 'I'm not The Settler now, you understand Jess? This is just play.' The boy nodded.

There was a silence: a few seconds of absolute quiet as Wes fixed his attention on the bottles. Then, before the boy could blink more than twice, the gun was out and a rapid succession of shots smashed into all the bottles in turn, throwing glass into the air in all directions.

Jess whooped and clapped and Wes handed him his gun back. 'This your gun, Jess?'

'No . . . it's Pa's. I borrowed it as he's real sick.'

'No son, Pa is not so sick . . . he's come round. You better get back in the house now! Give me the gun!' It was Lizzie, and her frown showed her displeasure.

The boy ran home, and Wes took the sting of her anger. The lecture lashed at him for minutes, as he tried to mumble an apology. 'Guess I better leave,' he said, finally.

'Wes, you have to understand, Jess has had to live with a father who cuts no slack. Did you know your brother was a tyrant? Oh yes, I can handle him, but I'm glad he's not my father! I have to work hard to keep him a measure civilized once he starts laying down the law on the boy. Sometimes I fear for what Jess might do. He's temperamental. He can change in seconds, like a game of poker. By the way, that gun . . . he's not supposed to have it. But I know he runs to somewhere safe with it, and I'd never tell Sam or he would thrash the boy. . . .'

'Well as I say, it's best if I go for now. But just keep Jess here as much as you can. I know one thing: he's a very talented shooter! Let's pray he never has to use that skill in anger, Lizzie. As for my big brother, when's he's feeling better, I'll have some words with him about giving a little, easin' up on the reins sometimes instead of always diggin' in the spurs.'

Lizzie put a hand on his arm as he walked to her. 'Wes, he needs to live more easy, that man o' mine. Sam acts like a church minister with a whole wide world of sinners to save. . . . Just promise me you'll watch out for the boy, please?'

'Sure. But again, I'm sorry. Tell Sam I'll come back when he's better.' Looking into her eyes, he could see a deep sadness, the kind that comes with a quiet sacrifice. She had given his brother her youth, her devotion and her love, and maybe he wasn't worth the investment. He had always been out for himself, and hadn't changed.

She squeezed his arm and managed a look of understanding and indulgence. He rode back to town, but with a worry nagging at him like a hungry dog at your coat-tail. His brother was a man heading for some large kind of misery if he didn't change. He was always stubborn, but now he was stubborn with a cause to fight. That was dangerous.

6

Ed Moran was feeling good. For once he was left alone for a while in the office and he looked across at the pride of his business: the Babcock printing press. He had always dreamed of being a writer, and he wanted to be in charge of what he put in print. As he saved the cash and set up his first paper, he dreamed of the best steam press, and here it was now, the heart of the little empire taking up two wide rooms in his main street home. There had been revolutions in the trade, mainly when wood pulp came along to replace the old rag paper. Yes, he thought, with that machine and his brain, the frontier could be cleared of some of its lies, its ruses, its downright swindles. The worst thing was that as the law was not able to reach into the new scrub towns and the half-made civilized ones, there was nobody to set things right, to shine a light into the rottenness at the core of the men who tended to be drunk on the little power they had. He had one of these sorts now, clearly in his sights: Ben Argyle.

He then looked at the front page of his new edition of *The Courier*. Bill Brady would not like it. Neither would the marshal. But that was too bad. The place needed stirring up to have some idea of how bad it was at looking at the mirror and seeing what was wrong with it. There was a sickness deep in Dalton, and its symptom was greed. That was the line he had taken in the front-page piece. 'The Problem of Loose End Yet Again' was his headline. Then he followed the words with a moral lecture. Argyle was to blame. All right-thinking men knew that but they were too yellow to say a word against the man. Well, the new edition would knock home a few unwelcome truths for the men sat in the jail like fat toads on a lily pad. Oh yes, he read the words of the leader to himself: *With the latest wave of crazed vermin from the south infesting our fine community, we look to the law for strength, and what do we find? We find a man totally unsuitable for the work and the trust we need to have in our justice and morality. All good citizens of Dalton knew full well that almost half of the place is unsafe for decent folk to walk, and when the cow-men swarm in, bent on raising hell, all we can say, from our office on the main street, is bolt your doors and keep your daughters at home . . . The law will not protect them. . . .*

That would surely stir things up. He thrilled at the thought that he had thrown a fox into the chicken run. Now it was time for a whiskey and a few moments of satisfaction. Any minute the Unity Men would be here – his fellows in the group that was set to change things in the town. They had started as just some friends who met together to stand in the way of the plans of Ben Argyle to run the whole town. He had now become so power-crazy that the Unity was aiming to do more than simply write for the paper.

They arrived together, with a buzz of chatter, and after some handshakes and back patting, they sat down around *The Courier*'s editorial table, as Ed called it, and Pete Maleno, as always, spoke first. With him and Ed Moran were Doc Pater, a lean and somewhat cadaverous man who reputedly lived an ascetic life, free of drink and beef, and then there was Cal Coover, who was the son of a rich man, and who hung around the bars of Dalton doing nothing more than being seen and playing cards.

'Gentlemen, here we are, at I reckon the fiftieth meeting of the Unity Men.' Maleno began, 'We have achieved a great deal, I suggest, in making life uncomfortable for Argyle and his lackeys. But I called the meeting because he's tightening the rope. Not only has the man sent his men to beat up Ed here, but he's doing what I dreaded ever since Emmy and me set up the Equity. He's playing a dangerous little game some call Wreck and Save. I been limping all day, and I got bruises on my bruises. It's just the latest in his reign of fear, Moran. I'm asking for ideas . . . and for help.'

'When he's in need of some medical attention, I'll

be unavailable,' Doc Pater said. 'You see, gentle-men,' he continued, 'we're dealing with a man who knows no morality. He wants to own everything and push everything, so as he's the law around here, how do we stop him?' He was tall, grey-faced and severe. It went with his responsibilities, as he ran the under-taker business as well as mending broken bones and treating fevers. Coover joined in, with a more active suggestion. He was every inch the rebel, with a buck-skin jacket and long fair hair. His boots were made especially by the best cobbler and leatherworker in the county, and his swarthy face suggested a rugged plainsman. Yet he wanted the world to think he was a poet and a sensitive soul, writing pieces for *The Courier* on the world of literature and art. 'They give us trouble, so we do the same. Let me hit back, you men. The way to do it is from behind, or in the dark, anything that can't be tracked and seen. Fact is, I've written satirical pieces on the man, and I've joked about him, but it's done no good. Same applies to your leaders and features, Ed. He laughs it all off and carries on bullying anybody weaker than him. Now he's got Brady in town.'

Ed went to fetch a bottle of whiskey and filled glasses, talking as he passed the drinks around, except to the Doc, who declined what he called 'liver poison'. Ed agreed with Coover, but summed up his opinion with the plain statement that harassing Argyle's men was a good way to get killed.

'Well, we can't give in. Now he's started this . . .

what is it, Pete?' Coover asked.

'Wreck or Pay. He aims to call it insurance, and it is, because Argyle refrains from destroying everything you have as long as you pay him regularly. Kind of *crooked* insurance.'

'Hmm. Brutally smart and very, very wrong,' Ed said.

'Gentlemen, we have Sam Galway behind us. We have the men who aspire to make this town equal the best townships back east. Surely Sam and his friends can find a way to beat down Argyle?' This was the Doc, trying to be constructive.

'I've tried to show the world how rotten the man is,' Ed replied, 'but it's time for more than words on paper. We need to catch him out crossing the line, have some evidence, and bring in the law . . . I mean, the *real* law.'

'Oh Ed Moran, you're so innocent!' Coover said, 'There's no real law here. We can only beat the man by strength. All he understands is power – power equal to his own!'

'Well, my good friends, Sam Galway needs to be on our side one way or another. I'll try his brother, who just came here. Maybe Wes Galway will help,' Ed said, and saw that the others all responded with humour and comments. 'Sure . . . I read your piece on him . . . The Settler no less. With him on our side . . .' Doc said.

'Yeah, but the point is he wants no more of that life,' Pete added, 'He's staying with us just now, though he's going to work with Steiner out at Three Mustangs. Word is that he's done with fighting injustice and standing with the little man. You did the man no favour printing the article on him, Ed – folks think he's still going to help them out. . . . Why, every needy person, every wronged and hurtin' little nobody is gonna want him to set their lives right.'

'Well we're little men, in front of Argyle, and we need a man like Galway,' Doc said. 'Though history tells us something valuable – that if we stand together, we can't be picked off. It's when we stand alone that the bastards can win!'

'All I know is I got to pay out a hundred dollars on Friday or . . . well, The Lord only knows what I'm in for if not,' Pete said, grimly.

Ed thought for a minute, then said, 'But I'll speak to Wes Galway. It's worth a try. Meantime, I'll keep on printing insults and accusations and see how he reacts! We got to prick him like a horsefly.'

'Well sure, but keep a pistol handy for when he comes through that door, Ed.' Coover laughed, with a dark shade to his words.

Lydia Steiner's homestead was something of a curiosity, as Wes could plainly see as soon as they rode into the gateway on her buckboard, with her old servant Henry at the reins and Wes's Appaloosa tied on behind. It was a grand, almost palatial house, with three floors and enough fancy trimmings outside to satisfy a European prince. There was not so much land: just a paddock, some land given over to corn, and then stables and a barn. Lydia had been explaining all the way out there that she was surviving, but it was all more show than substance. 'I still have the wardrobe and enough clothes to cover an army, and there's silver in those rooms that would decorate a palace, but as Henry will tell you, we have plenty of dollars but no workers to do things . . . thanks to Marshal Argyle, who wants us out of here. Right, Henry?'

Henry, wrinkled and leathered from a long life, hunched forward as he gripped the reins and complained incessantly. He was made of blood so mixed a man couldn't make out whether he was maybe Apache or maybe Mex, or maybe an English peasant in his origins. 'Yes Miss,' he spoke in a scraping, rasping voice, 'If I was a young sprat I'd be movin' on through cold fear of the man, but there's such a thing as 'llegiance and I'm the only honest man this side of Missouri.'

They stopped the chat when the buckboard pulled up and a dog started barking from somewhere. Henry saw to the business of opening up, feeding the hound, which looked like a wolf, and rustling up some food. Meanwhile, Lydia toured her home with Wes in tow, and he was bunked up in her husband's room. 'There will be plenty of clothes . . . should fit you well I'd say.'

'I can't wear dead man's pants, ma'am. Truth is, I ain't seen a room for so long afore I booked into the

Equity that I've found sleep difficult. Maybe I'll fix up a spot in the barn.' She tried to talk him out of it, but failed. Lydia soon learned that she was employing a man with his own mind.

Henry had a meal on the table and all three were soon aware of how hungry they were. The old man filled Wes in on the situation. 'Young fella, if you had a ounce of sense you would ride on out of here right now . . . nobody wants to come anywhere near the Three Mustangs. It's a ghost house. I'm right, Miss Steiner, don't try to deny it. The law wants you out and they've been patient for too long. Any day now that rotten lawman going to come in here and burn the place down, with us in it. You mark my words.' He spat out some food and then gave it to the dog, who was loitering, waiting for scraps.

'Ignore him, Wes. 'Course he wants us out, and 'course he's got numbers on his side, but I've now got The Settler on my side! You heard of this man, Henry?'

'No. Should I have done?'

'At last, somebody who's never heard of my heavy past . . . it hangs on my back like a sack of bricks, and I curse the day I let Ed Moran tell the world about me. But now I see that there's just you two here, then I can't see how you can win. In your place, I'd leave and head north.'

Lydia sighed. 'Wes, you need a lesson in basic facts when it comes to folks with roots. I take it you never had any. How can a drifter know about roots? Wes, this place can't be sold. It's crammed full of valuables from my husband's life. That lawman drove him to madness and to death, and I'm left with enough possessions to open up a store, but it would all be stuff for rich easterners. You see? So if I took off north, I would lose everything that could not be loaded in a wagon. I could take plenty of cash, and maybe buy a small place somewhere . . . but my life has been here. . . .' She was near to tears now, 'my life and the men I loved . . . and I'm *not* giving in!' Henry swiftly moved across to her and comforted her. The dog licked them both in sympathy. Wes felt her emotions flooding the atmosphere. She loved the old place and its memories.

'Yes, ma'am, I can see that there are very dear things still here to remind you . . . that is, things you could not leave . . . and well, I'll do my best, as your manager . . . But I have to tell you, I do know about roots. I tried to put some down once. I lost everything . . . careless, I guess.'

'What kind of roots?'

'The human kind . . . a woman and a child! Don't ask nothin' more, please ma'am.'

'Wes,' she said, responding to his request after looking at the change in his face and the pain in his eyes, 'I might not have long left here, but I'm going down fighting, and, and I'm honoured that you are with me, for as long as we have.'

'He's a complete fool, Miss Steiner. I seen some fools in my time, but this man beats 'em all, comin' here where the coyotes gather outside waiting for death . . . man's lost his brains. You fight for the Confeds?' Wes shook his head. 'North then . . . the cowboys will hate you but the locals will not, mister. 'Course, that prig Galway, he'll hate you. He can despise a man just for having the wrong kind of accent.'

Lydia and Wes looked at each other and laughed. The old man's remark changed the mood utterly, and everything was lightened. When the laughing subsided, Henry asked what was so amusing, and when told, he started to chuckle, too. The dog howled.

The new job was destined to be some trial of strength, and Wes knew it as he bedded down in the straw and sacking that night, having attended to his horse, who had earned a good feed and a warm blanket.

7

The next day, with the weather being warm and welcoming, Wes was up early and took a look around the place. The more he saw broken fences and peeling paint on walls, and the more he saw the fields overrun with weeds, the more he saw that here was something for him to do, something completely unlike knocking on doors to instil fear into a rogue or smack a man across the face for his transgressions against somebody weaker than him. No, this was what his father would have called a trial of strength – one of his favourite phrases as he struggled to build up his trade in New York, down among the dirt and the alleys, the threats and the pushing to have a little more space to breathe. If there was one thing Kansas had, it was open space. It made you want to take a real breath and fill your lungs.

This was a trial of strength, and of the patience that had to come along with it. Then he was awakened from his thoughts by the sound of Henry's voice screaming out, 'Time to eat, young fella!'

The breakfast was filling, and was badly needed, and Wes downed several coffees with the eggs and bread before letting Lydia and Henry know his thoughts. He said, 'I been rootling around the Mustangs, and you know what? I guess I'll make a stand with you. You got tools for land work?' Henry nodded. 'Fine, well as from now I'm manager, digger, painter, roper-in and general sluggard.'

'But first you are going to town . . . here's a list. All this will be in your brother's stores.' Lydia passed the list over the table. They all managed a smile and all Henry could say was, 'There's always some fella with less sense than a hog going visiting an abattoir. . . .'

Someone else was in town, and he shouldn't have been. Jess Galway heard about the cowboys coming in, and his father was at the meeting in the Harmony about the railroad, so he had some hours to kill. Jess had the six-shooter, stolen again from the drawer, and he wore the closest garb he could find to what a cowboy might put on. All he could assemble was some old high boots and his second-best vest, which should have been thrown away. But he had the gunbelt and the gun slotted in with no tie. Now he bided his time and went around keeping out of the light. By mid-afternoon, he had watched, from shadowed spots, as Texans rode in and swarmed into the sporting houses and saloons, and there was one little party that caught his eye. This consisted of a tall, well-made man of maybe twenty-five and two smaller men who acted and sounded younger. From their talk and their whoops of pleasure, he concluded that they were drunk.

When the tall man took out a rope and started whirling it around, accompanied by the shrieks of his partners, people stopped and stared; those walking along the street walked wide and gave the Texans plenty of room. Then, crawling along in front of them was a man whose gait suggested inebriation, and he was singing to himself. The tall man gave a chortle of pleasure and sent the lariat so it fell neatly around the man, and the rope was pulled tight. As the Texan pulled on the rope and dragged the victim towards him, the man yelled and cursed, which made the cowboys laugh even more loudly.

Suddenly, Jess sensed a movement to his left and someone darted into view. The man sprinted right at the Texan and punched him straight on the mouth. He fell down, and struggled to get to his feet. Only then did Jess see that it was his uncle who had arrived on the scene, and now the other cowboys were reaching for weapons. One took out a huge long knife and lunged at Wes, but the arm was parried and in a second, Wes had the man in a hold and threw him roughly out into the dirt. The third man turned and ran. Now the tall cowboy was going for his gun but Wes kicked it away, and they fought.

The tall Texan held himself as if he knew the boxing ring, ready to take some revenge, while the drunken victim crawled away and, as a crowd gathered, someone helped him move out of the trouble spot.

Wes and the man stood eye to eye, and they waited for the first move; this came from the cowboy – a hard swing of a fist aimed at rapping into Wes at the throat. That was always done with an intention to disable and threaten life. The man was real mad now. He had been outfaced in front of those who had worshipped his strength. But the swinging arm was blocked as Wes took the force with his forearm, and then swung his right hand into the man's belly. As he staggered, a second blow hit him on the chin and he was out cold.

The crowd applauded. Someone called out, 'The Settler! The Settler beat the scum!'

Wes had been in the stores, and Henry was carrying bags and boxes onto their wagon, but he stopped to see the fight, along with most folk who were walking around the main street. As people patted Wes on the back and called out, 'Stay and take a tin star!' some more cowboys came on the scene, lifted up their big friend, and were planning trouble when there was a shout of a deep voice, a voice of sonorous command, and Bill Brady walked up to the cowboys, with a band of his officers behind him, his presence and voice being enough to let the cowboys know that they should move on. 'You respond in any way to this and every one of you will spend a month in my jail, on bread and water. Got that?'

Everyone dispersed now, leaving Wes and Henry standing by the wagon. Brady took the opportunity to say what he had been planning since he arrived. 'I know you. You're Galway's little brother. Heard you were a drifter, so I suggest you drift on somewhere else. You're a violent man, and this is a peaceful town.'

'Who am I talking to?' Wes asked, insolently.

'William Brady, I'm the law while these Texans are here with cash to spend. They move on, then I move on. Meantime, you're gonna leave.'

'No I'm not. I work for Mrs Steiner at the Three Mustangs, as this good man will confirm. I'm a citizen of Dalton, as much as any of these good folk watching you now. I suggest you go and find criminals, Brady, and keep your distance from me.'

Jess relished every second of this confrontation. Uncle Wes was standing firm, unmoved, looking the big man in the eye, and his hands were nowhere near his pistols. It was all about courage. Jess was longing to snatch at his own six-shooter and let the big bully have a taste of lead, but for the time being, he had seen his hero. He had witnessed Wes Galway doing what his story said he would. The man was afraid of nothing and nobody. *He* was going to be Wes Galway.

Wes needed a drink, and he needed time to think. Leaving Henry with the wagon for a while, he was heading for the Equity when he saw the sign over the

Harmony, SAM GALWAY LECTURE. This could not be missed. He was soon standing at the end of a row towards the back, where the seats had run out, and there was big brother Sam, clearly better and back at his best.

'Ladies and gentlemen, I say again, the money has been raised, the line will go ahead. Most of you surely now have the bonds. You are investors not merely in a railroad, but you know what . . . you are investors in the future of this magnificent young nation of ours! Yes, you are! Stand proud and bold, you Dalton people, you Kansas venturers into the new world! Stand bold and brave, I tell you!'

There was a pause as he looked around, taking in the applause as his name was called out. Then he changed tack. 'Consequently, there is to be this new line . . . now I need to talk economic facts here. A new line needs the best route. It needs the support-ing facilities. You can't just build a line across a chunk of prairie and do nothing else except maybe have a patrol to keep out Indians and bandits. No, there is building to do. The best sites need to be acquired . . . now I have to tell you that two or three such sites are still not available. No . . . it's a shame I know, but even with all your money and your backing, there are still obstacles. Yes. It's true. Another reason for this meeting is to inform you all that Marshal Argyle . . . where are you, Marshal, show yourself . . . come out here and explain!'

From somewhere deep in the crowd, Argyle

walked out. When he walked slowly past Ed, Coover, Pete and Doc, he received some very black looks. They had resolved to stay together, to fight back as one, and they were going to start at this meeting. Argyle walked to the front and stood next to Sam Galway. It was plain to anybody that the two men were close, utterly in cahoots, and their movements and looks said so.

'Now good people of Dalton, I thank Mr Galway for giving me the opportunity to speak today. I wish to stress the importance of sweeping away the old dead ruins along the track to Abilene. There are some folk who just will not step aside and allow progress to be made. I find that hard to compre-hend and I'm sure that reasonable minds like yours agree with that. I mean, I represent the law, and I can tell you that what goes hand in hand with law and order is a society all in step . . . there's no room for radicals, for dissenters, for the faint-hearted and the obstinate, like the man who runs our paper here, Mr Moran. Yes, he's sittin' there like some sore on the backside of this individual we might call Mr Future Dreams. I believe in Mr Future Dreams . . . and I can see from your faces that you're in his family too. . . .'

Cal Coover could take no more of this. He jumped to his feet and shouted out, 'How about tyrants? Despots? Where do they figure in the future dreams, marshal? I s'pose you shove them aside as well?'

Sam intervened here, raising a hand and calling for sensible questions, not bad temper. It was the cue for all four of the Unity men to stand up and start snapping at Marshal Argyle. Ed Moran led the attack. 'Folks, you all know me. This excuse for a lawman has already thrown some mud at me, for no good reason, and my question is, to both of you future dreamers, are you allowing that this glorious happy future has a place for good honest criticism and judgement? That is, may a man disagree with you and not be black-balled?'

Pete, Doc and Cal all added a little pepper to the situation by howling similar sounds of displeasure, and Sam answered. ' 'Course, 'course there's a place for nay-sayers. History teaches us that the great achievers, the builders of the future societies, they had dogs snapping at their heels. . . .'

'So now we're dogs?' Ed shouted.

Wes was silent through all this, but now decided to stir things a little. 'I'd like to ask the marshal why he beat up Mr Moran when the poor man was just deliverin' material to my brother's store?' This had the effect of Sam turning to Argyle and looking him straight in the eye, as if the shock of the statement had turned a friend into an enemy.

But there was no time for an answer. There were shouts and gunshots out in the street and the whole assembly rushed to the door in a stampede, leaving the speakers to stare in wonder, caught in mid-flow. Someone called out, 'It's Brady and his boys . . . and a bunch o' cowhands, head to head.' The crowd went out, now cautiously, and they stayed close to the walls of the buildings along their side of the main street. Wes went along with them, and he saw Brady and some police dragging a man out of the GUS stores. Brady called out, 'Thievin' scum . . . Texan no-good Southern shit . . . bring him along, boys!' But in the middle of the street, a way back, the cowboy's friends were shooting and hollering, so that the lawmen ducked and scrambled for cover, leaving their victim lying still now in the dirt, keeping low and flat, hoping to stay below the bullets.

The crowd suddenly saw an influx of cowboys from behind the ones already there, and the volume of fire doubled, then trebled. Argyle rushed out past the crowd to run to a position behind Brady. It was escalating so that it was going to be a full-scale fight between the men fresh from the trail, letting off steam, and the police. Wes, deciding what he could do to help, heard a voice behind. 'Uncle Wes, what do we do?' It was Jess, and he had his hand on his gun, ready to cock it and join in the chaos.

Before Wes could do anything, a buggy swung into view, coming around from the east, and it was plain to see that a woman was at the reins, with an old man next to her. It was Emmy, returning from a trip out visiting, and in an instant, the firing stopped. Wes rushed out, jumped up beside Emmy and took the reins, shouting for her to get down, along with the old man, who was the Equity's long-serving barman and general servant. Wes took a hard pull on the reins and the horse, who had been about to rear and give in to a storm of terror in his breast, was eased and quietened.

Bill Brady walked out, towards the buggy, and called across to the cowboys. 'Now you men, let's call it off and there will be no action taken. Your man is going to my jail, and he'll be treated fairly.'

The crowd decided to walk out and stand behind Brady, and everybody turned and left at the other side of the street. Brady, who had Wes down as a marked man, found the words to thank him, and Argyle now rushed out and went straight for Emmy Noone, putting an arm around her, though she pushed him away.

Jess, seeing all this, put his gun away and had to disappear into the shadows. Uncle Wes was in the heart of trouble again, as usual, and he would need a partner, a sort of shadow. Jess Galway was going to be that shadow, starting from now, he told himself.

8

At Three Mustangs, it was the evening meal and Wes, now at last changed into some new pants and shirt, though still choosing to live outside, was more acceptable to Lydia and Henry in their life of civilised talk, eating and reading that filled their quiet lives – at least, their formerly quiet lives, as now things were changing fast.

Henry had something on his mind and decided to stir things up a little, as he had been noticing things in the few days that Wes had been with them. 'Now Lydia, my dear boss, you've had a man around the place now. He's mended a fence and cleared filth out of a dozen places where there should be no filth. Now it's been a long time since a young feller was busy around the place, instead of my ancient creaking body, so has he passed his trial?'

Wes smiled at this and waited eagerly for her answer. 'Well I can recall the usefulness of a husband, of course, but we've managed pretty well, old friend, for some time. But I have to say, Wes, I can now see how quiet life has been. We've gotten used to our routine, and of course, I'm not blind to the fact that the Mustangs has been slowly crumbling around us . . . though thanks for your efforts, Henry, old friend.'

The truth was, though she would never say anything, Lydia had been completely distracted from her daily chores by the sight of Wes working hard at every little job that cropped up. It was reassuring having a man about; the mere fact of knowing that a strong type, with a record of handling himself well, was on her side, in her pay, was better than any insurance policy tucked away in a desk drawer. But it was more than that. She had come to remember the feeling of having a man hold her, come near to her and offer comforting words when she was feeling low. Even in such a short time, she had noticed his little ways, his habits. There was something wild about him. Any reasonable man would have inhabited a bedroom. There were plenty of those. But he was only happy out in a barn. What a strange character she had brought in, but somehow a likeable one. There was something reliable about him: he was *capable*.

'Ma'am, we're comfortable, and the food is good. I haven't had talk like this for years, being out on the trail or scrattin' around in border towns . . . but every minute out there, working in the day, I can sense that Argyle could work his way into this place and ruin you. I mean, you need an army . . . not just me,' Wes said, between sips of coffee.

'Wes, we'll merely take each day. Argyle is surely not so ruthless that he would do anything illegal. He'll be pulling in lawyers to beat us away . . . we'll lose in the courts, not in a battle!'

'Wes, I told her she's too innocent . . . the man is capable of being ruthless, I know that and you know that. But the Steiners came from a place, somewhere in Eastern Europe, where the Russkies hated them, so your family knows all about standing up to bullies, Russian or otherwise. I wish you would see sense and move on, Miss Lydia.' Henry was aware that he had warmed up into a lecture and settled for shutting up and refilling the coffee cups.

'All I know is, based on past experience,' Wes said, 'that past a certain line on the map, this country turns from good manners to Sodom and Gomorrah. I'd feel happy seeing you sell up and move somewhere safe. I'll talk to my brother. . . .'

'No you will not!' Lydia rapped out these words, her face flushing with anger. 'I wanted you to kill Argyle . . . they were my first words to you, but Wes, what you don't know is how deeply in my heart I feel the urge to get even with this viper! He pushed my man to death . . . he might as well have put a gun barrel to his head and pulled the trigger! I'm going nowhere until I've beaten the monster who pretends to be a man of the law. Wesley, let me tell you a little about the Steiner I married. He was a man of principle, and a man who knew how to make money and be safe. His race have been hounded from every rotten scrubland the world pushed them to, and they learned to survive like rats cornered and desperate. My husband worked every hour of the day, saved and saved, went from a barrow salesman to a store holder, and learned how to take some risks, then he came west, joined in with the visions, before the Homestead Act, back in the fifties . . . and he built this place for me. It was no more than two shacks when we came. Then my family came to help . . . and died here . . . so I say again, I'm not leaving this place until I get even with Argyle . . . and I'm sorry to say that your brother has the same stink of rotten soul in him . . . there, I've said more than enough!'

Wes was more than a little impressed and his expression showed it. 'You have a warrior in you, ma'am. I've never seen a woman with more dynamite in the fighting spirit. All I can say in reply is that I'll stand by you. Can't say more 'n that. I always did stand by a person who was up against injustice. I'm the innocent one, too, as I came here thinkin' I could just change my life, nice and easy, into a sodbuster or a carpenter . . . a man with a trade of some kind. How wrong can a man be! But be prepared for a David and Goliath situation, ma'am.'

'The bigger they are, the harder they fall, Wes Galway,' she said, serious and solemn.

Henry and Wes looked at each other, and their

silence expressed more unease than a thousand words.

In the Equity at the end of a more than usually eventful week, it was far from quiet. Emmy and Pete were well aware that while the Texans were in town there was a chance for profits to be boosted somewhat, but nevertheless Pete stood at the door, vetting and checking, weighing up the characters of the men who turned up and wanted cards and whiskey. He let in the older men, though on the trails these numbered no more than thirty. He knew that filling a place on a night with card players was generally less risky than allowing any kind of drinker to come and hang around the bar, heading for trouble and wanting it as well.

Emmy had been so shocked by the gunfight that she had been shaken up very badly, and had needed plenty of tender care for the day after. However, now she was back in place, making sure the hotel ran smoothly. Pete had asked her not to get back to work so soon, but work was the best cure, she said.

Emmy was skilful at making men welcome, and she could charm the most boisterous drunk, but without some forethought, a saloon bar could soon fill up with the undesirables and the outcome was invariably a type of anarchy well beyond the law's ability to handle it and restore peace. This night, though, she had three or four men, one of them the trail boss, close around her like bees to honey, and her smile was beguiling them for the night, as they imagined that, for a moment at least, they might win her favours and affection. The trail had been long and hard, and some had almost forgotten the touch and smell of a woman. She knew all this, and she treated them to the feminine company that they might have recalled from far back.

Pete kept an eye on her and was there to help if matters developed into more than smiles and jokes, but on this particular night, as it was Friday, he was expecting the Wreck or Pay men. Argyle was a man of his word, especially the unwelcome items in his vocabulary.

Another man who knew very well that it was now Friday was Ben Argyle, and he had asked Brady to come and see him in the jail office. It was time to take stock of things. Argyle sat back in his chair, with one leg on the low table and the other resting on the floor. He was chewing baccy, spitting lumps out between his words, and Brady was standing by the empty cell, trying to keep still, when he was bursting to get back into action as there was so much to do.

'I don't like it, Bill. I don't like all the obstacles. You know, I'm coming to hate that damned word, *obstacles*.' Ben said this while starting to rap his fingers on the table edge. 'There's Ed Moran and his cronies, like stubborn old asses . . . then there's that Steiner woman, digging in her heels, and worst of all the man you came to eliminate for me, Bill. You're a might slow with this one.'

Bill Brady decided to grab a coffee, though it was stewed like wet dirt, and he sat down, to glare at Argyle as if he was defending himself against a legal accusation. 'Look, Ben, we go back a long way . . . you know me better 'n your own right boot. When I say I'll do somethin' then I do it. The case is these Texan cowhands, they've been keepin' my boys real busy and I've had to . . . well, you know. But your Wes Galway Settler man, he's livin' on borrowed time. Could be that by next week, they'll be buryin' the man and old Doc Pater, well he's liable to be polishin' a casket.' He spat out the coffee.

'Well I hope so. I'm paying good money, Bill.' Argyle spat out the last of the tobacco. He stood up and walked to the window, squinting outside. 'See, it's taken me five years to take most of this town. Just a few pockets of stubbornness left. Now, I have to tell you, in confidence, that I have plans for Mrs Steiner and her damned Mustangs ruin of a homestead that would maybe seem a little extreme, but it's the only way. Then I'm squeezin' the property owners so that they'll give in and sell. I need you to stick around, Bill. I can't fix things with the usual boys. They got drinkin' habits and unsuitable temperaments for the kind of work I offer them, you understand?'

'Sure. I'll hang around a while. First little chore is rubbin' out this Wes individual. His card is marked, Mr Argyle. Just one thing though . . . get some good coffee in, will ya?'

*

93

While they were chin-wagging, across at the Equity, Emmy was with her crowd of admirers, and a new face had joined them. It was a weathered old hand who had seen maybe one too many long trails, and he had a grudge against the world. He arrived mean and got meaner as the evening went on. Even worse for Emmy was that the man started making remarks about her. Matters started tightening somewhat when Emmy asked about the men's lives back home.

'Well I don't really have a home, ma'am . . . the sky is my roof I guess. Never had a woman like you to go home to. . . .' One man was saying. Then the new-comer chipped in with, 'You wouldn't want to come home to this woman . . . she's been around like an old coin. Passed around and dirtied with wear, you could say.' Heads turned to look at him and the other men, calling him Charlie, told him to mind his manners. But he smiled and laughed to himself. 'Don't you remember me, Bella Rosa . . . from the Silver Moon?'

'I think you've got the wrong woman, mister,' Emmy said, though inside, though she didn't recognize him, she knew that her less than pretty past was being dug up for entertainment. The man reached out and squeezed her around the waist and she slapped him, to the amusement of his friends. But Pete, sitting with his Unity Men, was over by her side, swinging a fist before the man with the insults could recover any composure. The next thing was that the man reached for his pistol, but before his hand could reach any leather, a bullet slammed into his shoulder and he yelped in pain. Everybody stood back, making a space, and Pete's was the gun with some heat in it.

Pete said, 'Now Doc, get this fool patched up. Everybody else, I apologize for the drama, but it's all over now, so get back to the cards and the throat burners.' The wounded man, vowing vengeance, was helped out, Doc directing the men to take him to a back room.

Emmy held Pete's hand and touched her cheek with it, before kissing it. She spoke to him with passion. 'That was some scum from the past . . . I'm through with men, like I'm through with the past, Pete Maleno, but you've just proved that not all of the male race are no-good wasters who just want to own you and ruin you . . . thanks, from the bottom of my heart. . . .' She kissed him on the cheek, but she couldn't go back to being charming. She retired for the night and went upstairs to hide from the noise, and more so from a shiver of fear and regret that was wracking her. There would always be men like that, bringing up the memory of the woman she used to be when survival was tougher than today.

Downstairs, the Unity Men were full of talk about Emmy, as she had been the centre of attention as always, but this time in a risky, dangerous way.

'She is one rare dame, Pete,' Cal said as he sat with the others, 'You asked for her hand?'

'Cal my friend, nobody will be good enough. I've

asked her twice and been turned down. Argyle has asked her . . . she turned him down. I reckon it's best to leave be now. She's more than happy entertaining these lonely cowhands and putting some colour in their day.' Pete waved for more drinks.

When they were all settling into their beers, except for Doc, who was with the wounded man, and normality was restored, Cal Coover said, Gentlemen, it's Friday. It's pay-up day. I guess you all knew that?'

Pete explained what was going on and Ed responded with, 'I'd almost forgotten. We're not paying a dime, are we boys?' They all shook their heads.

'Maybe Argyle will forget,' Cal said, and the others said, in no uncertain terms, that he was always a man of his word, even the lousy words, and most of his vocabulary was of that description.

'Got the bullet out and saw to the blood,' Doc said as he re-joined them. 'Let's hope he has no friends of an unforgiving nature.'

'He's a Texan,' Cal said. 'A dog pisses on their bedroll, they tell the world and hunt him down, to cut off his pizzle!'

They were enjoying this, with some loud laughter, when Max and Slug came in, with enough meanness on their faces to turn a drunk sober.

'Well now, I heard there's been some trouble tonight – anything to do with you, Mr Moran, as you can stir up a fight in a monastery.'

The four men around the table remained silent.

Their faces showed an implacable attitude. They were not giving an inch. Max sensed this attitude but carried on bantering. 'Now you better listen, Moran, with your written lies and libels . . . and you, Maleno, you ain't fit to run a rotten shack, never mind a fine hotel like this. With this in mind, you need some insurance in order to survive, just keep your mangy head above water, because you know what? The flood is comin' and you will be drowned. Or it could be a storm, or one of these here earthquakes . . . or a revolution. They come around every so often. The long and the short of it is, and I have to spell this out because you're all short of common sense, that you put a heap o' bucks in my hand or. . . .'

'That's a threat then, Max?' Ed Moran asked, cutting off his menacing statement. 'I can write in my paper that we were threatened . . . that you are committed to what's known as extortion.' The others nodded and made supportive sounds. Max turned to Slug. 'Slug, my friend, I think these gentlemen need a lesson in basic law. Like for instance, who is the law around this town. You know that, Slug?'

'Sure. Ben Argyle, marshal, appointed all proper and constitutional I'm sure.'

'Appointed by his friends and victims more like!' Cal Coover butted in.

'Cut all the women's chatter and reach into your pockets for the dollars. Do it now.' Max's tone changed and his face turned from fake humour to open aggression. But the four men remained still

97

and silent. People around the bar had started to listen in, and Max's last words were loud enough to attract a few more bystanders. The last thing Pete wanted was another fight in the Equity. He had already made enemies, and his place was starting to feel no different from the dens and dives south of the rail line. He thought of paying up, but Doc seemed to read his face and grasped his arm, saying, under his breath, 'No, Pete, no. . .'

'Fine, you're not payin' up. Well I'll report this to the marshal and I'm sorry to say he'll not be pleased.'

'Max, I've known you a long time,' the Doc put in, 'In fact I mended your cracked skull once after that confrontation with the Hubbard boys. Now I know that your skull is real thick. But I'm starting to think that your brain maybe leaked out that day I operated on your skull. Thing is, we haven't broken any law . . . none at all. You are breaking the law in truth, with your threats . . . so I'd leave now before all these good people throw you out!' There was a noisy response from the crowd. Max heard Slug say that they better leave, and he said simply, 'We're going, but this is like to be the biggest mistake you ever made – even bigger than thinkin' you could run a hotel. Seems to me you only take orders from the skirt. You let a woman boss you, so there's nothin' about you that we're afraid of. I feel sorry for you, aimin' to stand in the way of the law. The graveyard got plenty of men who tried that. . . .'

'Just get out,' Ed Moran snapped. For a second, Max's right hand moved over his gunbelt but he thought better of it, and he and the men behind turned and went, to the cheering of the crowd.

As he reached the door, Max kicked out at a table and knocked an old-timer backwards so he was flat to the floor. 'I'll see you again, Maleno . . . in hell!' he shouted.

9

Wes rode into the GUS ranch knowing that his brother would not be too happy, but as he dismounted and left his horse at the stable, it was Jess who ran out to meet him. 'Uncle Wes . . . you came! I was hoping you would. Ma says you upset Pa . . . and Pa's none too pleased. You disagreein' with him?'

'He needs somebody to talk against him. He's too full of himself, Jess. He always was. You keep on stirrin' him up, as he gets too full of his own importance. Now how's the shooting practice?'

Jess gave no answer but started to play, faking a grab for a pretend gun and then pointing his finger at Wes, who pretended to be wounded and staggered forward. He rubbed Jess's head and said, 'Now Jess, supposing a man does point a gun at you, from close up. And you're unarmed, or taken by surprise . . . what do you do?'

'Run like a jackrabbit!' Jess giggled with the fun of

100

the thought.

'No. The opposite ... if you run, he's got the whole vista stretching out before him and there you are, a target in the middle. No, you dive for his feet. Then he has to adjust. Chances are you'll have him down before he can move his barrel down to you.'

'Let's try it,' Jess said, 'You draw on me.'

'Fine, but make it quick. We don't want to be seen. . . .' Wes drew his pistol, and said, 'Hands in the air mister!' Then Jess dived for his uncle's feet and they were soon mock wrestling in the dirt, laughing and screeching with delight. Wes let Jess take him in a hold, letting his arm be twisted back, when there was the sound of hands clapping. They stopped, looked up, and there was Sam, with Lizzie by his side.

'Well, brother Wes, the man who spoke against his own kin! The man who always took against anything his big brother did. Now he's teaching a boy how to be as feckless and stupid as he is himself. I suppose you want Jess to be hitting out on a wild trail, turn into the next Settler? That what you want?'

'They were only fooling around, Sam,' Lizzie said.

Wes apologized, dusted off his pants and hat, and was asked to come inside. Jess ran off to give his pony some exercise.

In the house, Lizzie sensed the bad atmosphere like some storm brewing. Both men were uneasy, sitting at the table, with coffee put in front of them. Sam looked every inch the political candidate, being

101

for all the world knew a lawyer or a banker – a man who was going places. He was still in lecturing mood. 'Wesley, I can see that you get a kick out of crossing me, just like you did when we were ten. I can recall the look of pleasure on your face when you outed me, teased me, crossed me again, and you felt that little triumph. Well you know what I got to say now? I got to say who's the success? Who is the coming man here? I'm looking at my little brother and I'm seeing a drifter, an aimless man, a shadow. You have no roots, no place of your own, no plans. Now I hear you're working for Lydia Steiner out at the Mustangs? Well, I guess she pays you in kind, as you're used to living!'

Wes could have been angered by these words, but he knew, as in times long gone, that Sam was a man who spewed out words smoothly, but they were empty words. He was a man of straw, and the locals would surely find him out for what he was. There was no need to say much, apart from defending Lydia. 'Sam, you couldn't be more wrong about Mrs Steiner. She's a good woman. She pays me in cash. I work hard to improve her place, which is near being a ruin, to be honest. You got no call to label her a whore. I would say you're bitter. You're sore that she will not befriend you!'

He knew he was right, as his brother's face slightly reddened. Yes, he had hit a sensitive subject there. Sam changed the subject now. 'Look, Wes, you were at the meeting. You understand the situation.

102

Steiner is from the past, she lives in a world that has to shift out of the way. You know, I read a good deal about the old world, about the world her family lived in. Dances, coffee houses, polite conversation and servants. Her husband, in his head, was still in that world, and that ruined him. She will go the same way. That old world, Wes, it's dreamland, it's what exists in the tales for children . . . I beg you, quit the work there and come and live here, be *my* manager!'

'Nice try, Sam. You always wanted me to be your servant, your right-hand nobody. Well it won't work now . . . I like it at the Mustangs. I'm needed. I can see that this old world has a place still, and I'm standing in Argyle's . . . and your . . . way, brother.'

Sam tutted, blowing out a sigh in frustration. Speaking more quietly, almost to himself, he said, 'Wesley, Wesley, open your mind for once, see me as I really am. . . .'

'I saw who you really are at that lecture, brother. You stand with the lawless lawman. I hope you're happy with him and the murders on his hands.'

At this point, Lizzie came in from the kitchen. Wes noticed that she was wearing the cameo, and she said how much she loved it. She kissed his cheek and said, 'Sam, your brother knows what a woman wants . . . some consideration. Your brother,' she said to Wes, 'he thinks that a solid bank balance is enough. Could you teach him some courtship . . . with his wife!' She laughed at the teasing, and she laughed more when Sam was flustered and lost for words. She went to him and hugged him. 'I'm just ribbing you, dear! But this is such a lovely brooch.'

'Yeah, brother, it is lovely,' Wes said, with a wry smile, 'You know where it's from? It's from that old world that Lydia Steiner lives in!'

Sam could only offer a nod and a sigh. 'Just come and work with me . . . foreman. I got staff for the stores, but I need a good man here. What do you say?' Lizzie joined in, and Jess, who was now coming back inside, heard the question and said, 'Yes Uncle Wes . . . come and live here!'

'It's tempting, nephew. But I have obligations. There's a lone woman, facing big trouble, and I want to be at her side. Sam, you have all the power you need right here, including this fine son you should be real proud of.'

'I hear you, little brother. I can see now why you became The Settler. You always needed a cause, always wanted to back up the underdog, the little man, the one who stood against the majority. Strange that you didn't fight for the Confeds . . . and I wouldn't be surprised if you joined the Texans for the next trail.'

Wes nodded and gave a little bow towards Lizzie, saying, 'So glad you liked the gift, ma'am.' Then he left, pleased that his brother knew his thoughts now, clear as day.

For his part, Sam watched his brother go, and inside, there were dark thoughts. Wes had chosen to be a problem for Ben Argyle, and Argyle's problems from past years were all lying under the earth in the Dalton graveyard.

Pete Maleno had done the chores for the morning and was carrying some old bits of furniture that had been broken in the previous night's troubles. He had a broken chair in his hands and was at the deep end of the alley between the Equity and the offices of Ed Moran's *Courier* when a voice called out his name. He turned to look and a shower of bullets cracked into him, some shattering a part of the chair, and some slamming into his chest. As he dropped the chair and fell back, another bullet buried itself in his forehead.

In his office, Ed Moran heard the crack of the shots and rushed out. He saw the still body of his friend and went to him, looking right away for signs of life, but there were none. There was no breathing and no pulse. He had been riddled with bullets, and it was too late to do anything to save him.

Others came to the scene, and soon a man ran to fetch Emmy. She was deeply distraught, falling on the body and hugging her friend, weeping over him. Men stood around, some whispering about the cowhand Pete had shot. But there would be a time for that kind of talk when Pete's body had been carried inside and the Doc came to start his work as undertaker. But of course, when the body was put on a long table in the hotel, Ben Argyle had been called for and he had arrived, with a comforting arm for

105

Emmy, but she looked at him hatefully through her tear-filled eyes and darted out a hand, scratching his arm, like a furious cat. 'Get out of my sight, Argyle. You know who did this . . . you were his enemy, you sick piece of work . . . someone take this excuse for a lawman out of my sight.'

But the marshal had to be there and he explained, mainly to the others, that he had to ask questions. Emmy was taken to somewhere quiet and Doc and Cal tried to soothe her. Ed was listening to Argyle ask his official questions, noting the tone of voice, gauging whether or not the lawman was responsible. But if he was, then he put on a convincing performance, appearing to be concerned. He asked for a description of the man who had insulted Emmy; he asked if anyone present had threatened Pete. It was all seeming to be the right approach, and those standing around thought their marshal was ready to start his enquiries. But Ed and Cal later put their ideas to Doc as he finished the first tasks and handed a death certificate to Argyle. 'It's perfectly clear,' Cal said. 'We didn't pay up. This is our punishment. God help the rest of us if this is what Argyle does when you cross him.' They all agreed that the hotel should be closed for a while and they felt better to know that the Doc had sedated Emmy, who had been sobbing so much that she was capable of nothing else but curling into a ball moaning Pete's name.

It was near midnight by the time the remaining

three Unity Men sat together in the *Courier* office and tried to come up with some ideas to protect themselves. Doc took the lead. 'Look, this was nothing to do with that cowhand. They wouldn't do that. When they sobered up, they would see that the drunk was in the wrong, reviling a woman like that. No, this was no Texan cowboy vendetta. This was our old enemy Argyle, and we have to watch our backs.'

Cal was more than usually agitated. 'I think we need to be careful . . . but not panic. Stay together, that's the way out of this.'

Ed was thinking of the speech that Sam Galway had made. 'Now boys, listen. You recall the speech and the reference to what stood in the way of progress, all that wordy rhetoric . . . well, I think we can assume that Argyle and Sam Galway are close as two stage horses, reined up together like one beast . . . the test is, how do we prise them apart? Because if we can do that, we'll be stronger.'

But Doc was aware of the threat in the streets. 'Look, there's Brady, as well as Max and the barbarians hanging around him. Remember that it's Argyle who hires and pays Bill Brady. The big man will do anything the marshal tells him to.'

'So what you're saying is that we got enemies coming at us from all sides?' Ed asked.

'That's about it.' Ed reached for a cigar, which he did when he needed to think a little deeper, and he paced around the room. The others could only feel the panic of their minds, now trapped in black thoughts of bullets or knives coming at them from any corner when they were alone and vulnerable. Finally, Ed said, 'Look, we're vulnerable because we're not fighters, used to this kind of threat. But we know a man who can deal with the situation. We know Wes Galway.'

Doc sighed. 'Oh, the poor man. He comes here to change his life, stop the war he appears to have been fighting, and the whole place needs him. Near everyone in Dalton wants him to fight for them! You heard of Jack Sheppard?' They shook their heads. 'Well he was an English criminal who specialized in breaking out of jail. The crowds in London loved him. No matter what he done, they cheered for him, and they came to see him and ask him to be friends . . . his criminal career was his biggest asset! Well this is Wes Galway. He's out with Lydia Steiner and I heard he's real peaceful and content mending fences. Now you want to hire him. That what you're saying?'

Cal said, 'You put that very well, but yes. The answer is yes, as no other man around this town is so useful with a gun. I heard he's killed nine men.'

'I heard twelve,' Ed added. 'But even Wes can't watch every hired killer who stalks around the place, waiting for one of us to walk down an alley like poor Pete!'

Doc seemed to have a touch of enlightenment. 'Now my friends, wait a minute. Who or what could be Argyle's weakness? Because every man has a

108

weakness . . . like Samson's hair. I'll tell you what . . .
Emmy Noone. The man adores her. You must see
that the main reason he wants the Equity is to be
with her . . . which by the way gives him an even
better reason for wanting Pete dead. Now what I'm
saying is that I'd bet every penny I had on the Equity
and Emmy being safe, untouchable in fact.'

'You've lost me, Doc,' Cal said. 'You sayin' we hide
under her skirts?'

'I'm saying that Argyle wants the hotel. If we take
it, with Emmy on our side, then it would be a fortress
against the man. It would be the biggest obstacle in
the way of both of them, him and Argyle.'

Ed was not entirely sure what was being suggested.
'You mean we stand in there, armed to the teeth?'

'No, don't be ridiculous . . . we own it. We buy
shares in it . . . we become partners. Emmy will agree
if we tell her all this.' Doc smiled with satisfaction,
and the others appeared to understand, and they
liked the notion.

It was a long time since Wes had enjoyed a game of
cards, and he rode into town with some relaxation in
mind. The Equity being closed, he asked what had
happened and was told about the killing. There was
nothing in his mind to link the death with Argyle,
and he just moved on to find another saloon. He
crossed the line to the southern streets of Loose
End, and in a matter of minutes there was that noise
again, and the stink. The rank side of a cow town

always had that stink of work, sweat and fear. So much food and so much trail leather was on sale in every little corner that the sheer crowding of the unwashed losers and tricksters seemed to trap in the worst of humanity. You went into these unchartered side streets with care.

He found just the place: a pianist played an out of tune instrument in a corner, and six card tables were packed and noisy. Women fixed on a line of men at the bar, squeezing them of dignity and cash, and some were being led upstairs to have all their pockets and bags emptied.

He leaned on the end of the bar and called for a whiskey. 'I want the real stuff, not somethin' you made in a bucket this mornin', you understand mister?' He said to the greasy barman, whose apron was soaked in months of filth and waste. When the drink appeared in front of him, he asked who ran the place and he was told 'Not Argyle that's for sure. We never see the law in here, except for that big man brought in for the trail end hell the Texans create.'

Wes walked across and took the place of a man who was too drunk to carry on in a poker game. The other players didn't smile and never asked his name. He was just included in the game, without a word after he put some dollars down. But scarcely had the game started than there was a shout of, 'That kid again . . . get him out!' Wes turned, to see two or three burly men around someone smaller, held in the middle of them, and he was shouting out 'Uncle

Wes!' Wes ran over and grabbed one of the men, taking him around the waist in a grip and throwing him across the room, where he cracked his head on the wall. Another man turned and swung a fist, but this was blocked and then the attacker was hit hard in the belly. As he lurched forward, Wes struck again with an uppercut to the jaw. Then there, standing defiant like a cornered rat, with his hand grasping his six-shooter, was Jess. 'I saw you, Uncle Wes . . . and I saw *him*. . . .' He pointed across to the bar where Max was staring at them both, looking innocent as a little child as Jess said, 'He was about to pull a gun on you, Uncle Wes! Then I called out for him to face me. These men were his partners . . . .'

'You know this kid?' Max asked. 'I almost killed the boy . . . he threatened me, you understand, mister. But course, you and me, we got a score to settle.'

'He was going to shoot you, Uncle Wes,' Jess said as Wes took hold of him and led him outside to safety.

'By God, Jess, don't ever come into Loose End again, you hear? What were you doing here anyway?'

'I followed you. I'm your assistant, your *compadre*. Like in the stories.'

From the door of the saloon, Max and his men gathered as Wes walked Jess back up into the safer street. 'We got that score to settle, Galway. We'll meet up again.' Max yelled, above the noise.

When they picked up Jess's pony from the stables and started riding out to Sam's place, it was time for a lecture. 'Look, Jess, first question: why were you there?'

'I was watching your back, Uncle Wes. I can see that you're working alone, as you always did, like it said in the newspaper. *The Settler works alone, then he can't blame any other man if he fails to deliver.*'

'What? Are you quoting this word for word, Jess?'

'Yessir . . . that was in the story book my pa brought back for me when he went to Topeka.'

'Well Jess, listen up now. I need to tell you about weapons. You see a man doesn't carry a gun without a proper sense of its danger and misuse. It's a small thing but a powerful one, and a man has to rein in his temper, retrain the urge to use the thing . . . you follow? It's for protectin' your life, not swingin' around like some toy. You see?'

'You don't want a partner? I'm fast enough to be real useful. You need someone to cover your back.'

'Sure, and I thank you, nephew. But you could have gotten shot to rags back there, and what would I tell your beautiful good ma? They would both blame me.'

Jess was quiet for a while as they cantered real steady, and Wes let the boy's brain do some serious searching into that essential subject in life, the morality of the gun. Eventually, Jess said, 'Now I see, Uncle Wes, it's a responsible thing. But you see, I didn't shoot. If I had, then the Lord help them men!'

There was little hope of changing the boy. His

head had been filled with tales of adventure, and the worst of it was that he was a hell of a good shot. Wes was busy thinking what story he might spin for Lizzie and Sam when he got the kid home. It would have to be a convincing lie.

10

The delegation arrived at the GUS ranch in the early afternoon. They were expected. It was Sam's chance to confirm his status with them, as their local man – the man who would get things done. Lizzie had prepared food and drink, and Jess had disappeared into a world of his own, well away from the corral and barns, to somewhere he could shoot at targets.

Sam liked few things better than such delegations. It meant that a man was worth some attention if a delegation called on him; it was an indication of importance. He wore his smartest Sunday suit for the occasion. They were generally in a hurry and that was desirable too, as they tended to leave you with a job to do. He had dealt with such outfits many times: committees, councils, brotherhoods and associations. It was all the same outcome; work to be done.

They were men in dark suits and short on smiles

or pleasantries, and they walked in step, each with a valise: all four of them said the required compliments, mostly to the woman of the house and some to Sam himself. Their leader was Charles Linder, and he was tall, thin and younger than he looked, as worry combined with liquor had lined his face and given him a mark that created a permanent frown.

Linder and the others did the shaking of hands, and they sat down for a light meal. Lizzie, playing the role of waitress as well as good wife, knew where to smile and how to please. She had always known that it was a woman's lot to back up her man, but inside the walls of that home she was in her domain, and every man knew it.

'Mr Galway,' Linder began, 'You know why we are here. The calendar for the progress to our new terminus . . . it's pressing. We thank you for your report, and I have some comments. These are mainly about the list you gave us of potential problems for the new line. Mr Galway. . . .'

'Sam, please. Call me Sam.'

'Very well. Now, Sam,' Linder said stiffly, not being used to anything but formality, 'Sam, you list two old-timers with shacks basically, and one ranch called the Three Mustangs. Now our usual custom is to offer a purchase. This has been done in the case of the single and rather aged men, and they have accepted cash. Now, a Mrs Steiner at the Three Mustangs, she has refused our offer. Are you acquainted with the woman at all?'

115

'I am. She's stubborn, stuck in her dreamy past and still thinks she's some kind of fallen aristocrat who needs to be a special case. The old world still inhabits her head. We need to find a way to remove it.'

'Well Sam, that is your duty. You know from our first liaison that you were appointed the local man for the railroad company. That company pays you well. We are pleased with your work so far, but now we must insist that you find a way to remove the woman. She has become what my father used to call the stone in the pony's hoof.'

'Short of blurring the line that defines the law, I can't see what gambit is open to us,' Sam said, his face showing how troubled he was inside. Usually he could face a problem and think of a solution, but this was seemingly beyond that.

One of the other men, who had not yet spoken a single word, said blandly, 'Mr Galway, when it comes to railroads, the law may be bent somewhat. Have you any idea how many people depend on this new line? We are talking thousands. Do you know how many businesses depend on the line? No? Well, a railroad head creates around a dozen other companies, all concerned with buildings, food provision, security, communications. . . .'

'Fine,' Sam cut in, 'Fine. I see your point. I'll find a way to effect Mrs Steiner's removal. It's a matter of sentiment of course, and sentiment can sometimes be more powerful than anything in politics or any speechifying and lecturing.'

'Good, so we understand each other.' Linder stood up, gathered some papers together, and nodded at the other men, who all followed suit. There were more handshakes and then they left, with profuse thanks spoken to Lizzie.

When they had gone, there was a look on Lizzie's face that showed how angry she was. Sam could read this, and at first he tried to make excuses and went to his office, but when he came out, she had not forgotten, but had saved up her words. 'Samuel Galway . . . I've always been proud of you. You have won your way from nobody to a man of achievements, a powerful man in Kansas . . . but as far as I know you've kept to the right side of the law. Are you going to tell me that you will evict Mrs Steiner by force?'

One thing Sam could do was lie. Cultivating a false exterior was a skill he had mastered, and after the initial worries about what his wife would think of him his ruthlessness took over and the acting began. He acted like the best thespian in Washington now, and slotted his best reassuring tone into his words, combined with an arm wrapped around his wife's midriff. 'My dear, you are to have no worries on that score. I know that you have a certain affection for Mrs Steiner . . . I know she has lost family . . . she is almost alone, I know that. You can rest assured that I will simply talk her into leaving, or should I say, relocating her place to somewhere well away from the noise and steam of a locomotive. Of course, we

117

are not barbarians, as they are in England. I read in the papers that over there the railway companies simply move in on people's private land and start digging ... just shoulder in and to hell with the owners. I read that in *The Times*!'

'Well I'm so glad to hear you say that, my dear. You see, you are so often silent, wrapped up in your work. It's so difficult to figure out exactly what is happening inside that skull of yours ... the brain that built an empire, of course, and that's wonderful ... but please don't become a brute like that marshal is reputed to be!'

He gave her another comforting embrace and spoke softly, 'My dearest wife, you know that I am not capable of such a shameless, unscrupulous action ... against a lone woman ... the very idea revolts me!'

She seemed placated, and both went to their chores. Sam was in his office after that, partly in a mood of triumph and partly holding off a terrible sense of shame that he could lie so. He sat at his desk, as he always did when trying to think. He was desperate to come up with some other method of talking the woman out of her land. Time passed and he was sweating and fretting with the effort of racking his brains. Surely there was a peaceable way? He lit a cigar, stood up, and walked around the room, and there he caught sight of himself in the long mirror, used to check his appearance before important occasions. He saw there the actor he knew he was: there he was, the man whose principles slipped and slithered like a rattler. There was that man, who could surely tread the boards and fill the air with the bubbles and fabrications of the tragic hero. Only, if this were so, what would be his tragedy? Lies, he had often been told, tied knots in the fabric of honour. The man in that mirror was a mirage, or maybe a ghost. Yes, he was the ghost of that young man who had journeyed west with the zeal of a missionary. It dawned on him that he could never find the good words again – only the devious ones, and he had now told his best, most malicious, lies to his own wife.

Where was that young man now? Lost forever, he knew. Lost, and the mission he once had was dissolved like a dried up spring.

11

In the Equity, Emmy was taking Pete's death very badly indeed. After a day or two lying low and weeping all the pain out of her at least so she could try to get back to work and life, the morning of the funeral came and Doc Pater took charge of everything, as he was used to doing. Most of the town turned out, and the new church, with the wood still smelling of nature's own juices and the sweat of the workmen, and Sam Galway gave the sermon. He had reached the point in his Dalton life when he was the man you asked for when a speech was to be made. He was a regular speaker for the Methodists anyway, and had strong views on everything, from wine to wasting the Lord's precious gift of time. His theme for the day was the dedicated man who changed his life, and he told Pete's life as far as anybody knew it.

'He came into town with a past he didn't seem to like and he never spoke of it, except that he had kicked and shouted at cattle down in Texas a while, then kept clear of the war. Seemed he saved cash and came here with the intention of owning something, of being a man of substance, and so he became . . . our thoughts go to his dearest friend in life, Emma Noone, who came to love the man, as we, his closest friends and neighbours did.'

Wes, at the back as usual, couldn't help but see himself in Pete's life story. He had drifted in just the same. But the problem was, he had no funds, nothing in any bank. He was a hired man, slaving for a wage. But at least he had turned down the offer of money in exchange for taking a life. Taking lives was what he wanted to leave behind, but he was being hard pressed.

He went back to the GUS homestead to spend time with his family, and to make sure that Sam hadn't found out about the escapade south of the rail line. Young Jess was taking more and more risks, and Wes saw that he was the only one who could keep the kid away from trouble.

At the Equity, after the funeral, the Unity Men knew that it was never too early to bring up the topic of the plan to own the place. Some hours had passed, and the hotel had been reopened, though Emmy sat still, just watching the world of gamblers and drinkers with a bland, bored expression. Ed saw that it might be the right moment for the important talk, and he took the others over to sit with her. 'Emmy, we've come to say something important. It's business, so if it's not appropriate today, tell us to get

121

lost and leave you in peace . . . but we think it's about survival.'

'Go on, I've done the grievin' at least for now. Though a piece of me has been tore out. By the way, Doc, thanks for what you done today. You're a true friend.'

Ed took the opportunity to raise the difficult subject of Argyle. 'Miss Emmy, ma'am, we had a talk about helping you here, and we know for sure that Ben Argyle wants this place.'

'Ben Argyle wants me for his little obedient wifey, but he can go and whistle at the moon for that. He's a man possessed, and I hate him.'

'Well,' Ed continued, 'I know it's a painful line of thought, but we're sure that Argyle is responsible for Pete's death . . . it's not the cowhands. Now, what if you had three partners, all investing in this place, spending time here, being around all the time to keep it safe . . . wouldn't that bring a certain peace of mind?'

Emmy looked at them all, her mind churning away, thinking about the implications of this request. She had always been in charge. The Equity had been the real embodiment of a dream she had had years back, when she got away from the sporting houses and low bars down south in New Mexico. She had vowed to herself to get out of that life, a life that dirtied her soul as well as her skin. The Equity was hers. Pete had been an investor and a sidekick. Now here were three investors. But of course, they were offering security.

'I'm saying yes, boys. We'll sign up a lawyer and make it official. Though I want the major share. Folk will still need to think of the Equity as Emmy's place, right?'

They each gave her a hug, and Ed told the pianist to stop the solemn tunes and play something from down on the border, where Pete's roots lay. 'You know what Emmy,' said Cal. 'How about we make the back room where the entertainment goes on into the Pete Maleno Suite? We'll put a sign up!'

It turned out to be a funeral day that everybody remembered, as it was the day that there was a celebration as well as a string of short speeches and toasts in Pete's name as the day wore on into evening. Outside, down the street, Ben Argyle and Bill Brady stared at the Equity, wondering what could be going on. They expected only solemn music, strains of a violin maybe, and a sad hymn. Someone walking past, as dusk fell, told Argyle that the Unity Men had moved in.

Unity Men, Argyle said to himself. *Who the hell are they?*

The next day Wes turned up at the Three Mustangs after a good time with the family, during which Sam had avoided too much preaching and moralising. Jess had kept to himself, and Wes hoped the boy had been turning over the advice about guns they had talked through. It was a heartening scene that met his eyes as he dismounted and appeared at the door of the home: Lydia was at the table, stitching a dress hem, and old Henry was cleaning his rifle. But the impression was soon destroyed.

'Ah, the foreman returns! You've come just in time to mend the lean-to door. It fell off last night in the wind,' Henry laughed as he said this, but Lydia was not so light-minded. 'Yes, and you weren't here when we had a little communication.' She held up an arrow, then took a rolled up sheet of paper and read from it: '*Steiner, leave by the end of the week, or you'll lose more than your home.* Pleasant little note, attached to the arrow. It was shot at me as I swept the porch. I saw someone ride away . . . it wasn't any Indian though. But maybe the marshal's paying warriors . . . Comanches, now?'

'Argyle's little game I think,' Wes said, feeling the mood drop real low. It was like something was weighing on the whole place, pressing the feeling of life in the walls.

When the table was cleared and they sat down to eat, she said, 'Wes, I been thinking . . . when I first met you I said I wanted a killer, right? Well you've told us what this lawman is capable of, and I know how he's hurt me . . . well, I got to thinking, strike before he strikes! What do you think?'

'I'm no hired killer, I told you that,' Wes said.

'I can do it. What have I got to lose? Life owes me nothing. I'm seventy years old.' Henry had changed from cheerful to deadly serious. 'I fought in the war,

124

lived on salt pork and cornbread full of weevils . . . been shot at and wounded, been half-starved . . . had a family and lost it . . . let me go and finish off this lawman! We know he's goin' to wreck this place. It's just a matter of time before he does.'

Wes gave him a hard look, searching his face, weighing him up for the nature of his real intent. It was a convincing appeal all right. The old-timer would be capable of that.

'You are surely right, ma'am. Argyle wants to reduce this place to rubble. I'd bet my life on that. But it's suicide to march into town and try to kill the man. He's surrounded by a small army of paid lowlife scum. One man can't stand against them. I say we stay here and wait, but be ready.'

'Be ready? How? You got the cavalry round the corner, mister?' Henry said, pulling a face in his expression of criticism.

'I'll think of something, Henry. There's always a solution to a problem.'

Actually, Wes had no ideas at all. It would need some hard thinking. For a while, the low mood was there, but something in Lydia changed her mood, and when they had eaten, she brought out a bottle of wine and handed out three glasses, then filled them, with a steady hand, now composed and seemingly free of the anxiety of earlier. 'Now my friends, there may be something of a mountain in our way, but in the end we have to live for now. The Steiner story is one of persistence. We hang on and we trust in God or Fate to haul us out of a hole. Now I have to ask you to raise your glasses, because it happens to be ten years since I first came, with my family, to this wonderful land called America!'

'I'll drink to today. It's all there is!' Henry said, drinking the wine down in one pull.

It was one of those evenings when stories were dug out of memory, and Lydia talked of her father and his life back east. Henry recalled his war, and then they both looked at Wes. 'Your turn, Wes Galway. I know nothing about you except what's been in the paper.' Lydia said. It was something Wes had no time for really, but he made an effort. 'Look, all I can say is that I saw the war as well, Henry. I was there at the start, at Manassas, when we made a bad opening, no real leadership. But since then, when I survived all the years of orders, bullying and threats that soldiering was, miraculously the bullets missed me and I went south . . . I got to know life with cattle and with Indians. At one time I could more or less speak in their own tongue to the Apaches. But if you're celebrating the Steiners, then let's drink to the Three Mustangs and the future!'

'Well I never heard a man so cleverly avoid talking about himself,' Henry said, 'but I'll drink to that.'

The evening turned into dark night outside and they tired. Henry went to his room, and Lydia saw that Wes was ready to go, too. But as he stood up to walk to the door, she took his hand and pulled him gently back down to sit with her. 'Wes, you know

126

what *lonesome* really means. It's a terrible word, that lonesome.' She stressed the word so that it was drawn out, sounding sadder than it might have been just rattled off in a conversation. 'You must have ridden thousands of miles, slept out under the moon hey? I'd wager than you have sung a few old ballads to yourself, out there in these God forsaken territories, am I right?'

'Sure I know lonesome. It can be a comfort. But it's a pain as well. It can be like there's a feeling that some shadow of yourself is there, hanging around, reminding you that you've left company, run away from society. I've done that. It's a two-sided coin, ma'am. One side is truly pleasurable. There's strength in it. The other side . . . well, it's like an illness, a great aching nothing in you.'

Wes was starting to think that this woman was someone special to him. He had never been one for close friends. He was happy with acquaintances. But then, women friends had been as hard to come by as a rose bush on the prairie. Now here was one who awoke feelings in him that he thought had died long, long ago.

'Wes, anybody ever told you that you can shoot words out as well as you can bullets?' She pulled him close to her on the one comfortable armchair that wasn't loaded with materials, from all the curtain-mending she had been busy with. But there was one curtain length around the back of the chair, and she brought Wes's strong body down onto it from the arm of the chair so he lay across her knee, and she kissed him.

'You don't want to be in that cold bunkhouse tonight, Wes Galway. There's this thing called a bedroom . . . it has a bed in it. You remember what a bed is?'

There was no time for an answer. A rap on the door and someone shouting Wes's name put a freeze on the moment, and Henry came downstairs, wearing only his pants, grabbed a pistol and opened the door, which was bolted and locked. There was Sam Galway, and he shouted out, 'I've come for Wes . . . is he there?'

Henry let him in, and Sam had a look on him like a man facing a stampede. 'Wes . . . we're needed in town. The Texans have started a battle!' There was no time to waste. As they rode into town, Wes had the full story – or as much of it as Sam knew. 'A rider came out to us, said the cowhands had decided to hit back . . . seems the man shot by Pete was the son of the trail boss! Well, we got trouble too, brother . . . Jess is in town. Lizzie says he rode off around dusk after we ate. I was in the basement, too concerned with my own affairs as usual . . . poring over a damned railroad map. . . .'

When they reached the edge of town, there was no doubt that there was big trouble. They were north, and so they could see a rough line of Brady's police, strung across the main street, all keeping safely behind a rough barricade of boxes and

128

barrels; they were under heavy fire. Then from the walkway by the Equity, there was gunsmoke from inside.

'Get the horses in the stable . . . my man is there, from the stores,' Sam said, and he grabbed a rifle from his saddle before the two brothers ducked and scrambled around the back of where the lawmen stood. Crouching, hidden in the cloak of night, Wes said, 'If we arc around, we'll come out at the middle of the Loose End streets. But brother . . . my heart wants to fight against you, not *with* you! The law here stinks rotten. I know that smell. Sure the law is a shifting sand around the frontier, but good men can stick a foot in and do somethin' . . . I'm fightin' for your Jess, you hear?'

With a shout of 'follow me' he ran forward, keeping his shoulders bent over, both guns ready to fire. Behind him, Sam had his Winchester .44 but its stock had been mended roughly. There was still a crack across it, and he hadn't used it in anger since he bought it four years back.

When they reached the fringes of Loose End, at the top of a long side road no more than a rough track with the breadth of an alley, Wes could see that they could get up a staircase along the side of a saloon and squat on a ledge maybe fifteen feet above the street. They went for it, and as they climbed up, all eyes of the cowhands were fixed on the north end, where the barricade was. They didn't notice the two men behind them.

'They'll be after Maleno . . . seems they don't know he's dead. But there's revenge in their hearts, so the Equity itself is in danger,' Wes said, keeping to a whisper.

Sam held up the Winchester. 'Wes . . . I never fired this thing. Is it reliable? I'm not a man of war, brother.'

'Well I never would have guessed! Here am I thinking you was a gunslinger . . . but what you are, my brother, is a father, and you're here to save that boy.'

'Where the hell is he, do you think?'

'Chances are he's in the same saloon he was in the other night, when he was backin' me up.'

There was a look of complete shock on Sam's face. 'What? He was here in this lousy place . . . and you knew? You didn't tell me?'

'You would have skelped the boy, and what would that have achieved? Now he's most likely in there . . . it's two buildings along on this side. We can make it there if we run for it.' They came down again to street level, and Wes aimed to cover Sam as he made the first run to the saloon. What was needed was a distraction, and Wes planned to shoot across the street at a sign hanging over a store. 'Give me that rifle, Sam. We'll find out if it's any good.'

He took careful aim. Lady Luck was on his side now, as there was a lantern behind, and it gave him enough light to see the target well. With two shots he could break the chain and the sign would fall behind the Texans on the far side. The first shot hit home, and the sign dropped to hang loosely off the hook. Then the second shot, and the sign dropped. A great, heavy lump of wood had scattered dust behind two men squatting on the corner of the store. Luck was with Wes and Sam, as the sign made other men run across to see what was happening. That gave them time to sprint forward and duck into the saloon.

They found Jess alright. He was sitting with the barman in a corner. The place was empty apart from them. 'Pa! Uncle Wes! What are you doing here?'

'More to the point, son, what are you doing here? You're supposed to be in bed!' Sam ran across and the boy cowered. The barman stepped between them. 'Hey, easy now . . . this young man should have a deputy's tin star. He saved my bar . . . and most likely my life as well. Some drunken cowboys burst in when all this trouble broke out, and this young man here, he stood his ground, hand to his gun in less time than I take to blink . . . and three of these steer-handlers turned and ran for it! He your son?'

'He's my pa. Good to see you, Pa . . . and Uncle Wes.'

Sam was impressed, and other thoughts now erased the anger inside. The main thing was that his son was alive. He could deal with the bad behaviour later. 'Now,' Wes said, 'we're gettin' out . . . the Equity is where we should be, to help Emmy and the boys!' As he spoke, a man burst through the doors, staggered to the nearest chair and then tumbled over it, clutching his chest. Then he went down and lay bleeding. The barman went to help, but took one look and then shook his head. It was more than Sam could tolerate for a second longer. Being anywhere in Loose End was being in the ante-room of hell in his book.

12

In the Equity, every man who could fire a weapon was at the windows or the door, looking out onto a scene that could have been from a battle in the war. Most of them had fought in that war, and they knew that once a bunch of wild-hearted men let off some rage, there would be casualties, and the town had only one medical man. 'Course, he was one of the men with a pistol pointed out at the street. The fight had started around dusk, as the cowboys had wanted the cover of night to move in, and now they had the upper hand.

Bill Brady had seen two of his men shot dead and he was calling them to fall back. The forty or so Texans were slowly gaining ground, and Brady had only five men left by his side.

'Good Lord, boys, we're fighting for Brady! What's happened?' Cal Coover asked the world in general. 'We hate the man. Let them rub him out for us!'

'You darn fool, Coover,' Doc put in, 'They're after this place . . . they're looking for Pete. He's the one they want . . . maybe we'll tell 'em he's dead!'

'You aimin' to walk out there and have a chat to them?' Ed Moran asked.

'Dodging bullets was not in my medical training, friend!'

They saw the worst news they could have dreaded. The police officers broke and ran. They headed for the stables and it was clear that they were running away, aiming to leave Dalton behind them. Out in the shade of the stores across the road there was Brady, Argyle and a gang of men in Argyle's pay, including Max and Slug. They began to move across the road, towards the Equity, and there was nothing those inside could do to stop them. When Argyle came in, with the others behind, he said, 'They're damned insane, these cowpokes . . . seems the man Pete shot took a turn for the worst and died . . . Doc, you patched him up?'

'I did, but there's all kinds of filth gets in wounds. The Texans are not the most careful and clean folks around Kansas. A man can die from the infected wound.'

'Well whatever killed the man, we got the blame . . . Emmy . . . Emmy. . . .'

She had now come into sight, from the safety of the back room. Ben Argyle, a man still smitten with her, but who had made her hate him, was asking for help. 'Emmy, they don't know that Pete is dead. If they knew, they would go.'

'Why should I help the man, boys?' she asked. The men were still at the windows and door, and they knew that the cowboys were coming closer. Ed Moran took the lead. 'He's right, Emmy. You been in the crossfire already. It appears that they got some scruples and wouldn't put bullet holes in a woman. Maybe you could talk to them?' As he said this, a voice outside shouted to them. 'You folks in there . . . send him out . . . send out the man who killed my son. Send him out and we'll leave. I'm sure you know that.'

Wes wasted no time. He went to the door and walked out into plain view, in spite of all the voices behind him begging him to stay put. He was only visible in the dim light from the hotel, but the Texans could see him. 'You boys, you need to know the man you want is dead. He was buried two days ago, and you were no doubt too busy washing dust out of your guts to know about it.'

'That's real convenient mister. Prove it.' The voice came back from the dark street.

'What do you want us to do . . . dig up his body and drag him out here to show you? You'll have to believe us.'

'Believe you lying nobodies in suits? Believe you fat moneybags, fraudsters and hucksters? No . . . I can smell a coward from a mile off, mister.'

Wes had met these situations before. It was a case of shout and bluff. Courage changed everything, shifted a situation to an advantage. He walked out to where there was more light. 'Cowards? That what you think? Well, see me walking out here, no weapon in my hand, speaking the truth to you. You just as brave, mister? You like to walk out?'

There was what seemed like a long silence. Then the man in shadows gradually appeared, standing facing Wes. They were just around fifteen feet apart. Wes decided to use the advantage and keep up the straight talk. 'Fine, now mister . . . I have to tell you that the man who killed your boy was Pete Maleno, and he was shot down in this here alley behind me. He was unarmed, killed in cold blood . . . and by the law. So you see, this side of that iron road there's just as much foul play as down your rough end. Only difference is, you boys can see the enemy. We take the enemy for friends and they take us down in our innocence.'

There were mutterings behind the cowboy facing Wes. He tried one more ploy. 'Now my friend, I been down Texas. I had a family down south there . . .I lived in the Pecos . . . I know that men down there, they got a sense of right and wrong that goes above or below the law, depending on the crime. I know that you can see honesty and you can see suffering. Well there's a woman in that hotel who lost her best friend, and his death was more on the wrong side of legal than anything you might have done tonight. I suggest you saddle up and go.'

There was another long silence and more talk

from behind, in the darkness. Finally, the voice was heard by all the defenders of the Equity. 'Mister, you talk sense. We've dropped some lawmen . . . they was bullies anyways, so no lamentin' these hired men . . . but I think you're exactly what you say. We're turnin' south on the morrow. Come on boys . . . fight's over!'

He turned, and there was the sound of a body of men all scraping leather as weapons were put away, and their tread filled the dismal street until all sounds died away.

In the Equity, the sense of relief was palpable. They felt like cheering, but when the Unity Men fixed their gaze on Argyle and Brady, the sourness was still in them: the feeling that something rotten had stunk out the night air.

'This is all down to you, Emmy Noone,' Brady said, a threat in his tone. 'I been informed about you . . . what you were. The dead cowboy, he was just fool enough to speak a few home truths. Now he's dead, and your man's feedin' weeds as well, lady! Now folks, you ever thought about this whore's name? Noone . . . kind of like *no one* don't you think? She's nobody. She's a sportin' lady with all her tricks and she's puttin' on the lady act in your town!'

'Brady, you and me, we're startin' to reach a point of no return. That is, I'm sensing that I'm surely gonna teach you some manners.' This was Wes, moving forward from the group of folks around Emmy, all facing Argyle and his cronies.

'What? You aim to teach me some manners? Let's see you try.'

Wes was enjoying the way his provocation brought some results. 'Now big man, you know what my grandaddy told me? He said the bigger they are, the harder they fall.'

'Very amusin', you stinkin' drifter, smellin' a decent place out. Let's test that theory.' He raised his giant fists, ready for a scrap.

'You know what else he said, Brady?' Wes raised one fist and said, 'You want the infirmary. . . .' He raised the other fist, 'or sudden death?'

The big man took a step forward and was about to throw a punch when Wes hit him hard in the gut. It stopped him in his tracks. The crowd moved back and gave them some room. As Wes came closer, Brady brought a fist up and caught him across a cheek, so he reeled back a little. Then as the big man tried to take the advantage with another intended swipe straight on the nose, Wes ducked and moved to one side, before cracking the man hard in the temple and then following through with the other fist to the man's chin. Brady was dizzy with the punches now, and worked hard to gather himself. He managed to land a kick, his boot hitting Wes in the midriff, but then Wes took hold of the foot and yanked the man back so he fell and his head smacked against the counter's solid oak.

Wes waited for the man to struggle to his feet

before he caught him again with a boot in the crotch, and then he took the advantage by giving two close punches to the head again. It was more than the man could take and he went flat out, cold as ice, sprawled on the floor.

Emmy and the Unity lot applauded and called out Wes's name. 'The Settler! Come on, the Settler! You beat the bastard. . . .'

Argyle, just for a second, thought about reaching for a pistol, but then thought better of it. 'Come on, fellas. Help him up. We're all finished here . . . but Emmy, I'm sorry for what this man said about you. He had no right. Reckon I'm employing the wrong type of man these days. We'll be going. But Sam, you and me got business, or are you taking the part of your violent little brother here?'

'Yeah, are you with me or not, Sam? I'm not clear on that,' Wes challenged.

'Wesley . . . I thank you deeply for what you did tonight. We all do. You brought my son out of that rotten den of fallen souls, may they rot in hell . . . but there is still law here. The cowboys who murdered those officers today will be brought to trial, right, Marshal Argyle?'

'Sure. Let's go.'

Sam went out with Argyle and his men, and Wes saw very plainly where his brother's loyalties lay that night. His greed for power and wealth was stronger than anything to do with the everyday folk, working to make a living in the dirt of a tough life.

When the place was clear of Argyle and his rough-necks, Emmy and her new partners sat down with Wes to talk through the state of affairs. Jess was taken home by his father and two of Emmy's regular customers, for special care. Lizzie would have been worrying real bad.

'Emmy, what that turd said about you . . .' Ed Moran spoke first, 'We don't hold that to be worth a bent dime. Just want you to know that.' The rest nodded and spoke their support.

Wes cut through any more side-talk with, 'Now, my friends, this has all been very exciting. But the fact is that Ben Argyle wants the Steiner place and he wants this hotel. Now that you good people all have a stake in the Equity, he's liable to fight unfair. Maybe he'll just take it and throw you all out. I guess Brady will want to get even, too.'

'He's a snake, that man . . . he'll plug you in the back, Wes,' Emmy said. 'Meantime, we can hold this place against Argyle. Don't worry about that.'

'Force with force . . .' Cal put it. 'If it comes to it, Argyle ain't the only one who can pay the Brady characters in this world . . . you got cash, Doc . . . and you, Ed.' They nodded agreement.

'Argyle is now restless. He'll have no patience left. That means he'll try something desperate. Question is . . . what?' Wes asked them. There was no quick reply.

Emmy, who had seen the lowest places in life and who had learned to survive when all the chips were down, spoke with assurance, 'My good friends, listen. Me and Pete worked hard for the Equity. Now, with you men alongside, we can keep it, and I'll pay hired guns to take on Argyle. He'll get weary of that. I think what we should really fear is his plan for Three Mustangs, Wes. Now I know that you've put in time and claimed a boot-hole there with Lydia Steiner. I think that's where he'll hit hardest. He doesn't care if it's wiped out entirely.'

Her words gave Wes a sudden, terrible awareness of the situation. He had been so occupied with rescuing Jess and defending the town against the possibility of complete anarchy that he had left the Mustangs to the back of his mind. 'You're right . . . Mrs Steiner had a warning yesterday . . . an arrow, with a threat on paper fastened to it. . . .'

'Then you have to protect it . . . now!' Emmy snapped, in a passion. The others agreed. 'We'll get out there, now. It needs to be a fortress. He'll destroy it, Wes,' Ed Moran added.

'Sure, and my own brother will do nothing to stop him! I never expected to find a man like that when I rode in here. But if you leave this place, then it's vulnerable. We don't have an army. I have to get out there . . . now!'

13

The next morning it was Emmy Noone who saw the urgency of the situation and decided to do something. She was at the GUS ranch by first light. The only way to save Wes and the Steiner place was to talk Sam Galway into action. She rode into the place and was walked in by the stable manager as breakfast was being cleared away, and she insisted on seeing Sam in his study.

'Why Miss Emmy, what a surprise! I think this is the first time I've ever had the pleasure of welcoming you to my home.'

'Don't give me your double-talk, Galway. I've come to ask what you're planning to do to save the life of your brother.'

'What? Save his life? Why all this sensational talk?'

'Because, if you're too stupid to see it, your friend Argyle is going to flatten the Steiner ranch and your little brother is stubborn enough to fight back . . . at odds of maybe twenty to one!'

'What evidence do you have for this, Miss Emmy?' He stood up now and remembered that he ought to act like a gentleman even in the presence of a fallen woman, who really, in his morality, was not worth the trouble of a curse or a spit.

'I have the evidence of common sense . . . based on my knowledge of nasty coyotes like Ben Argyle. You said yourself there are obstacles in the way of your damned progress . . . excuse my language!'

Listening at the door was Jess, and he heard enough to make it clear that there was a serious problem about to present itself to Wes. There was no time to lose. He was needed. Before his mother could do or say anything, he darted outside and sprinted for his pony. The only other thing he needed to do was steal a six-shooter, and he knew that the workmen would leave their weapons around the stables or the barn while they were labouring hard. He stalked around the barn, glancing at the shelves and gates, and at last there was a belt and gun, hung on a wooden gate-top. He snatched it and went for his mount.

In the study, Emmy was exasperated by Sam's blockish refusal to take her seriously. She had tried common sense; begging was out of the question. All that was left was fear. 'Fine, do nothing. But you will be burying your brother maybe even tomorrow . . . you sit here, like some old king . . . so proud of your mindless drive to kick the town into some strange paradise of money and things . . . you're no different from the cattle drivers, shouting, goading and pushing their steers into the pens, where they are surely destined for somebody's table back east . . . fine, stay here. I tried. But be ready for that funeral!'

She went out, in a passion, saying nothing to Lizzie as she came out of her room to talk. But Lizzie grabbed her sleeve. 'Emmy, wait! What are you doing? Why are you here? Has Sam done something?'

'No . . . he's done nothing and that's the problem. Let his brother's death be laid at his door!' She pulled free of Lizzie and ran out into the light.

Sam emerged from the office and he met the stare of his wife. Without a word, and simply with a certain look of accusation, Lizzie made her husband turn his head down to look at the floor. He could feel the weight of conscience – something he thought he had jettisoned long back – bending his will. Lizzie knew what Emmy had been here for; she knew that Sam had let her down, let them both down. 'I have always believed in you, Samuel Galway . . .' she said, simply and increasingly uneasily. 'Always trusted you to do what was right, and always taken your word. But I recall that you said Lydia would be fine, that she would be treated fairly. Now I'm doubting those words. Am I right to be doubting them?'

'Lizzie . . . there are forces at work, in the world of commerce, of tough business . . . forces at work, that

144

squash a man, crush even the best of men, and sometimes a man is in the grip of these forces and he can
do nothing. . . .'

'No, not if he's a weak, cowardly sort of man who
has brushed off his morals like dog hairs on his best
coat! I think you are that kind of weak man, Samuel
Galway. I hate you!' She ran to her own room, with
no idea of what she should do, and for a while, she
ran through in her mind what could be done to
help. Yet her words had had some effect on Sam. He
paced the room, then returned to the office, and for
a split second he caught sight of himself in that
mirror yet again. It seemed to prick his conscience,
and he raced for his key to the basement. Surely
there was time to do something? What was going to
happen suddenly hit him in a new, terrifying way. He
had nodded and agreed to something horrendous,
something brutally wrong. But there might still be
time to stop it. He darted around, looking for the
best of his rifles, and deciding in his head what he
would do if he met Argyle. That thought made him
pause. Christ! He would have to stand in Argyle's
way. That would be suicide. Sam Galway was not a
violent man. He had only once in his life fired a gun
in anger, and that was at a robber making off with
property at the first version of his Dalton stores. Now
here he was, fastening a gunbelt around his waist
and thinking about facing a man like Argyle or even
Brady – men who would place no value on a human
life and use their weapons as thoughtlessly as they

would feed a dog.

He stopped and started. He made ready and then he halted and thought again, and time ticked on. When Lizzie came out from her room some time later, the dark, hateful look was still on her face, only this time she spoke. 'You want to stay my husband? Get out there, take the men, and stop this!'

Now he had no choice.

If Emmy had known it, there was good reason to spring into action. The night before, at the end of the long day's events after the street battle, Ben Argyle and Bill Brady put their heads together, deep in conversation until past midnight. Brady was seething with rage. He had been brought down to the level of no more than a street dog, a cur on the road scavenging for scraps – in his mind at least, for he was a proud man who never let a grudge go cold.

'Listen Argyle, nobody else is to touch Wes Galway, you hear? Nobody is to hurt a hair on his head, except me. I need to get even. No man has ever insulted me so before, and I want to watch him die!'

'Fine, fine, now cool down, Brady, cool down. Things will happen when they will happen ... in good time. See, there's a lawful way to remove a problem, which entails a bunch of men in smart suits arriving, toting their valises, and they *negotiate*. That means producin' a deal involves too much jawin' and precious little doin'. Right? Now the word *negotiate* is one I detest. It slows down everything right and effective. Now this here Steiner woman, the world she comes from, that's a world where folks negotiate till the air turns brown with boredom. Then there's the other way to take care of a problem. That's why I pay you, Brady.'

Argyle had taken too much cheap whiskey and his brooding, hurt self came through moaning like a hurt child after a rough street-game. 'See, I paid you to remove Wes Galway. You ain't done that yet. I been patient. Very patient.'

'It'll be done, Mr Argyle, you wait and see.'

'It will, because I've organised it all. This is what's gonna happen tomorrow. Max and the boys, they'll make sure the Mustangs barn goes up in flames, right . . . then you and me, Brady, we'll be watchin' the front door for when Wes and that woman come rushin' out . . . and then, well, you know the rest.'

'Just a minute, no, I can't murder a woman!'

'No, you fool. We let her rush to the barn. But we kill the old man and Galway. You got it now?'

There was a satisfied smile on Brady's scarred and worn face. Life had battered him, but the deep lines still came out strong when there was something stirring his feelings. He was already imagining Wes Galway laid out on the earth, dead as a stuck hog.

The two men had no sleep that night. Argyle went out to look for Max, Slug and the rest, who were holing up in the stables, bedding down in straw. They were happy to have come away from the fight with the cowboys without a bullet hole in them. Argyle took Max to one side and gave his orders, slipping a bundle of dollars into his hand. 'There's another two hundred for you when that barn is a smouldering heap of ash. You understand?'

Max nodded, and his eyes brightened at the sight of the money, tight in his hand. Through the night, Max and his pals prepared. None of them knew the place, but one barn was like another. Everything in it would be alight before a man could take two breaths, and seven men, each with a light and some oil, could bring a wild fire to its height in no time.

Brady managed a nap, after checking and cleaning his rifle and six-shooter. His mind would not come away from the sick feeling in his guts that he had felt when he lay on the floor of the Equity, wanting to move a leg but being unable to, with his head thumping and dizzy.

Then, at first light, they all moved out, riding steady and straight to the Steiner place.

'You know the story of the Three Mustangs, Brady?' Argyle asked, as they rode side by side in the early light, ignoring the chill that invaded their bones. 'No? Well I was told that this woman's husband, he came here with these three horses, and nothing else. But he was short of cash when he needed a roof, and being a gambling man, he wagered on his best, quickest mount . . . a beautiful pinto . . . and this animal, it was like the wind. It was speed as well as stamina. Every man around the county took the challenge and tried his best against this pinto. They all lost and the Steiner enterprise was richer and richer. Now, when he dug in and built the home, he had his kin to help . . . two men who came out west after him, city boys. They were given the other horses. But there was a hex on the place. There was a disease that took the men and the animals . . . all of 'em except Steiner. He buried them all together and left directions for him to lie with 'em. So he eventually did. Lydia Steiner, she gave the place the name as, so I heard, some Indian magic man, he said the horses would ride the men to some kind of heaven . . . some great plain full of buffalo. Nice kind of baloney eh?'

'You should be a real good liar, Mr Argyle. You talk a story so well,' Brady said.

'Now you know what I plan to do, when the sun sets today? I'm putting up a new sign. It's to be The Three Doomed, as that's what they are, our targets for today. No room for feelings, Brady. We've messed about too long.'

14

At Three Mustangs, as far as Lydia knew, it was going to be another normal day, with normal chores. There was birdsong and there was the sound of a wind out there, but she put an arm around Wes and, though he was half asleep, she whispered, 'No more bunking out there in straw?'

'The war is responsible,' he said. 'Couldn't sleep in a bed after years on the ground, with just a bedroll from the saddle. . . .'

'Well, sleep . . .' she said, and kissed his eyelid.

The Kansas night held them all peacefully out of any troubled, threatening disturbance of the world they had made, but it was an illusion. Wes knew there was big trouble on the way, but you took every second of pleasure and fulfilment anyway. He had learned that.

Then the end of the night was coming. There was more and louder birdsong and the wind now rattled the roof a little; it was as if someone from the next

150

world or from the past was warning the sleepers in the Mustangs that they would soon face a storm, and it wouldn't be from the prairie.

The dawn stirred Wes, Lydia and Henry too, and the old-timer was up first, making some chow and coffee. He liked to say that he had learned how to make decent coffee from the poorest stuff, even straining the juice through a havelock, sewn on the back of the captain's hat. When the others came to eat, he was thinking of the war, which he did every time he did some cooking, as he had been the one the messmates turned to. 'Mornin' to you, and so it is. We have some warmth coming out there,' he said, pouring out some coffee as they sat down.

'I could have had a messmate like you . . . we existed on offal pretending to be coffee!' Wes said, but his humour soon faded. 'Look, I came racing back, and I'm as worried now as I was last night . . . we could see Argyle out there at any time. I'm going to have a ride around, just in case there are any signs. . . .'

'No, I've eaten and drunk . . . I'll take the sentry job,' Henry said, and he put his coat on and took his rifle, swinging it over his shoulder. He walked out and took two steps towards his horse when a shot rang out and, inside, Wes and Lydia heard him cry out in pain as he was hit in the chest. Lydia was for going out to him, but Wes held her back. 'No . . . no! They're already here . . . and there's smoke . . . smoke from the barn!'

151

Lydia pulled away from him, broke free, and ran outside, and Wes saw that she would reach the barn. No shots were fired. Lying low and squinting out through the window, he could see that the barn fire was well advanced. There was thick black smoke billowing out from the side door. He saw Lydia rush in. There were all kinds of materials stored in there, but clearly she was most concerned about the four horses in their stalls inside.

There was no doubt in Wes's mind that Argyle had arrived and soon these fears were confirmed as Argyle's voice called out, 'Wes . . . come on out. No point loiterin' in there, boy!'

It was an invitation to die. He knew that. He also knew that there would be other men around the back, watching for him to try a back-door run. He was trapped like a prairie dog in the open, staring at a hawk.

But the risk was there, and it had to be taken. He could only jump out, and roll down low for cover. The nearest spot to hide in was twenty feet from the door; a high fence with some rocks close to it. If he waited any longer, then the house would be torched as well. This was the day he had known was coming ever since he stood against Max and beat him up.

It was time for the old tricks to be brought up. He took a kitchen pan and threw it out of the door. Then, as shots rang out and bullets pinged against the tin, Wes rolled in a ball, hurling himself at the earth, and as he scrambled for the cover, more bullets came at him. He lay there, breathing heavy, his heart thumping so he felt it in his throat, and he expected more and more shots to crack. He had only his pistol in his belt, and he now took it, ready to use . . . But there had to be maybe six men, all with rifles, out there. It was time to pray.

All he could think about was Lydia in that barn, in the midst of the flames. He had no choice: he had to run again, this time in the open. It would surely be suicide. But he gathered all his courage and resolve and made ready to run for it. Then there was a shock. He heard a shot from further away, and someone yelped in pain – someone from where the attack was coming. The result was that his attackers were turning and shooting somewhere else. It was a second, no more, available and not to be missed. He sprang up and sprinted for the barn door. A voice from somewhere called out, 'Uncle Wes . . . dive and roll!'

It was when he reached the open door and snatched at the handle that some bullets finally came, ripping into the wood. He did dive, rolling again, taking his body into the doorway, as a bullet thumped into his right foot and he cried out in pain.

Emmy had arrived now, and she was behind Jess. She saw the situation and went to crouch by Jess. 'I have a rifle, Jess. You crazy kid . . . what are you doing?'

'I'm covering Uncle Wes. I'm his partner. I winged one of 'em. There's six. Two up there and four across the other side of the barn. I seen 'em moving into the back of the barn just now. They're waiting for Wes to come out . . . that lady, she's in there. The lady who owns the place.'

It was all making sense to Emmy now. Wes was his usual heroic self, doing stupid things, as he had plainly always done. Argyle and Brady had now taken cover and were circling towards where they saw Jess's gun-smoke. Emmy realized this and she urged the boy to move away with her, to hide in whatever hole they could find.

It was then that Max and his men came into sight, by the main door, and Argyle shouted, 'Get in there . . . shoot them both . . . make sure they're dead, then get out!'

The men did exactly that and went in, quick as terriers ditching for prey. Those outside could only crouch down and wait. But inside the barn, Lydia was with the horses, and she opened the doors of the stalls, cracking the horses out, and they panicked, racing for the open door, which was now fully open, as Wes had managed to kick the second door outwards. There was room for the horses to charge out, terrified. Max and his men just dodged them and came in, shouting for Wes.

They moved slowly, looking around. Above, they could see that there was not much time before the roof would fall, and there were flames engulfing the far stall. They looked around, hoping to see a clear straight, somewhere to walk slowly and spot their victims. Gradually, this became more and more impossible as thick smoke gathered and snaked its way into every pocket of air. Max and the others started to feel the bite in their lungs and they coughed like men choking in a fog, hacking and rasping as their lungs felt as soft as paper. Yet they pressed on, thinking that their targets would surely be dead now, and they could confirm that before rushing out. 'Just a few more steps, then we get out!' Max shouted.

Wes had staggered into the right stall, where he had seen Lydia, and he could tell that she was still moving. He inched nearer and nearer, forcing his wounded leg to move, to lift and propel him another few feet forward towards her.

'You just made it, Lydia!' Wes said, limping and in pain, but coming closer to her. She had breathed in too much smoke now and with a last call to him, she passed out and collapsed onto the straw floor, taking Wes down with her.

Their fall hid them from view, and Max and the men came in further, guns cocked and ready. 'Just find 'em, plug 'em and git out!' Max called, above the increasing noise from the burning wood around. It was then that part of the roof came down, smashing across the top of a stall and splintering. In seconds, the men were crushed, and they were stifled by the thick smoke around them, and hit hard by the intense heat of the fallen stall-side. Some tried to escape, but as they moved, they made more hot beams roll onto them.

Wes gathered every inch of strength and took hold of Lydia's body. He managed to carry her, one agonizing step at a time, towards the light he could see at the open door space. His mind was telling him that, if he reached that light, there were bullets waiting for him, ready to rip into his chest and finish him. They would finish her, too. So much for changing his life, he was thinking; so much for roots, and families. But he walked on, closer and closer to the light, with the heat behind him being more and more intense. He could feel the hot tongues of flame behind, almost licking his sweating back.

Outside, Bill Brady had crept around behind Emmy and Jess and Argyle was detailed to watch for movement at the barn doors. He expected Max and the others, but none came. Brady slithered close to the woman and young man, and he jumped on Emmy first, snatching her rifle and throwing it away, then shoving her away so she fell heavily. Meanwhile, as Jess was turning to him, he took him round the neck, pulled up an arm behind, and marched him out, towards the barn. Brady needed the comfort of a hostage held up tight to him, the best kind of armour. He knew what a perfect shot Wes Galway was.

Finally, Wes reached the light. He could sense that there was life still in Lydia and he spoke to her. 'You'll be fine, ma'am . . . I'll take care of you. You'll be fine!' As he reached the light of the door, he spun around, so she was protected and his back was facing

Argyle, a ready target. But Argyle saw Brady walking out with his young prisoner, and decided to make Wes suffer a little longer. 'Hey, Galway . . . see what he got here . . . that whore you seem to like so much. You carrying a corpse and about to see another one!'

Wes turned to face Argyle. He saw Brady walking out, Jess in his grasp. Argyle was laughing, and all Wes could think of was saving the woman and the boy. There was no choice but to drop her and shoot. He would have to drop his right arm down quicker than he had ever done before, and lift that pistol up faster that lightning. He was limping, so a crouch was an easy manoeuvre, and as he lowered himself ready to drop Lydia as gently as possible, he shouted, 'Jess, jump for the foot!' The boy pulled away, his head hit the boot of Brady, and the big man floundered for a second. Wes dropped Lydia, darted his hand for leather, and pulled the trigger so fast that Argyle was beaten and was hit in the face before he could draw. Brady had lifted his rifle now, but it had taken precious time to do that, and Wes's second bullet smacked into the big man's chest and he fell, hard and heavy.

Emmy ran to Wes, then to help Lydia. She was still breathing. Forever after that day, Emmy would tell folk that her life down in the rougher levels of society among killers and cheats had taught her how to save life as well as how to take it. She brought Lydia back to some colour, and now she needed a doctor.

'Uncle Wes . . . I dived down for the feet like you said . . . he couldn't handle the rifle!' Jess cried out. Wes nodded. 'Right, Jess. A man can't shoot a rifle down almost straight with the stock to his chin . . . not without takin' a while over it. You did good.'

There was what seemed at the time like a long silence, in which people said practically nothing, but looked at each other, and then at the ruin around them. Lydia was in no state to say or think anything, but if she could have taken the worst in, then she would have seen that everything was lost except the home itself. They had spared that. The strong wind was still blowing, and its wailing seemed to offer a lament for the sorrow around them. Wes spoke of Henry, and how he had been the strength behind Lydia, like a father to her.

Then came what would later be seen as the reason why Lizzie and Sam Galway were to split apart. The man who ran the General Universal Store might have been powerful but he was short on the kind of mettle a man had to have deep in his spirit. He had left everything too late.

Sam Galway and his workers were way behind and nothing they could do would have made any difference. The fight had gone to the end, without him and without any resources he could gather. They came riding into the Three Mustangs ten minutes after the last shooting. Sam saw his brother with an arm around Lydia, who sat up now, in the dust well clear of the burning barn, and his other arm around Jess.

158

'A mite too late, big brother,' Wes said. 'But I wasn't gonna lose a woman and a kid a second time. Now you can help by bringing Doc Pater to see to my foot. It hurts like hell!'

When, later that day, the survivors met in the Equity, Cal Coover asked Wes what he was going to do, now there was no Three Mustangs to work in. Wes, his leg patched up and most bones in his body aching, knew that Lydia was upstairs, in her bed, with the Doc making sure she was breathing better. With this in mind, he said, 'My friend, I lost a woman and a child once, through leaving them alone. I won't do it again.'

'So you won everything back!' Cal said.

'No . . . I lost a brother this time. I came to find him and all I found here was a shadow of that man. Yeah . . . that's what I lost, a shadow man. Lizzie lost him too, and she is the best woman a man could have . . . maybe except for Lydia and her old world charm!'

'But you got a partner, Uncle Wes . . . I covered you. I'll always cover you. If you're in trouble, look behind and I'll be coverin' you!' It was Jess, unobserved, in a corner, his gun covered over with a long coat, just like The Settler.

159